NEw
STREET
STORIES

NEW STREET STORIES

AN ANTHOLOGY OF NEW WRITING BY NEW STREET AUTHORS

Edited by Andy Conway and David Wake

*Sarah,
Enjoy*

See page 3.

Abigail see page 60!

New Street Authors

First published in Great Britain by
New Street Authors
Collection copyright © 2018 New Street Authors
All stories and poems copyright of their respective creators as indicated herein, and are reproduced here with permission.

More Canals Than Venice © 2018 David Wake; *Meet Me On The Corner* © 2018 David Muir; *Silver Star and Pumpkin Girl* © 2018 Tony Cooper; *New Street Blues* © 2018 Andrew Sparke; *New Street Station* © 2018 Dawn Abigail; *Pest Control* © 2018 T. K. Elliott; *Against the Odds* © 2018 A. A. Abbott; *A Window Cracked* © 2018 Guy Etchells; *The Six That Matches the Twelve* © 2018 Nicky Tate; *Philip's Decision* © 2018 Miles Atkinson; *The Regent* © 2018 Lee Benson; *Busking It!* © 2018 Martin Tracey; *Buffalo Bill and the Peaky Blinders* © 2018 Andy Conway.

Contents

Introduction

Publishing is changing beyond all recognition with the rise of ebooks, print-on-demand paperbacks and online retailing. With all the opportunities and perils that entails, **New Street Authors** formed in response as a collective of independent, self-published writers.

Launched in 2015 by founder members Andy Conway and David Wake, **New Street Authors** quickly established itself as a major player in the West Midlands independent publishing scene, providing readings and workshops at *Tamworth LitFest*, *Wolverhampton Literature Festival*, *Bristol Festival of Literature* and *Stourbridge LitFest*, as well as regular reading performances, signing events and launches in Birmingham.

New Street Stories is our first collection, a chance to showcase our writing and tempt readers to check out our published work.

So, come and look through future windows to past and present dangers; walk with us down The Ramp and along the canal; face monsters human and otherwise, and read what's new on New Street.

Editors: Andy Conway
and David Wake

For more information

newstreetauthors.com

More Canals than Venice

David Wake

The cuts meant the Council closed the Tourist Information Offices.

Ridiculous!

It made Jessica furious.

Birmingham had plenty of visitors and the city offered so much. There was the Bull Ring, the new library, the museums, the Rag Market, the Royal Ballet, the Sea Life Centre, good pubs, nice restaurants and... and... *it had more canals than Venice!*

She shuffled her paperwork again.

Martin Gillet, the arrogant pig, stood in the PowerPoint light wearing an expensive suit. He turned back to the graph of the deficit and he had such a tight arse.

It was her first job out of Uni – undergrad and masters, so she was behind the rest of her twenty-something colleagues due to her lack of experience – but the report was fine, neatly typed and she'd–

"Jess," he said. "Everything all right?"

"Yes, yes ..." God, his eyes shone.

"You look flushed."

"I'm... it's the light."

"Or is it my aftershave?"

The team laughed.

Jessica stared at the page as she felt her face turn into a tanning lamp.

Just concentrate on the report and it'll end. These meetings were–

Shit!

There was a spelling mistake. Not a proper spelling mistake, just a typo, but that apostrophe was in the wrong place. *Oh shit!*

"Let's just keep these disappearances quiet," Martin Gillet was saying – or something like that, Jessica was distracted: he had an English degree so how could the apostrophe be there and not *there*. Gillet's diction so perfect and educated, his teeth so white. "We don't want a statistical anomaly blown out of all proportion, do we? Three's hardly a crowd. It'll affect tourism, won't it, Jess?"

"What? Sorry. Of course, but if there's a danger?"

"Well, health and safety, obviously."

"Yes and–"

"No need to trouble the council with another, let's say... 'issue'. They've enough on their minds with this new Mayor."

"But–"

"We've specific instructions not to put anything else on their plate. You don't want the boss to be cross with me, do you?"

"No, but–"

"So, let's adjourn early to the pub. Everyone agreed?"

Everyone agreed.

Even Jessica, despite the several points still to cover.

But she should have insisted: particularly on Item 11, inter-departmental liaisons.

"You coming, Jess?"

"Yes, sorry, Mister–"

"Martin."

"Yes... Mi– Martin"

By the time Jessica had tidied her paperwork away in the drawer of her 'clean desk policy' work area, everyone had left. Except for Martin, who sidled over and leaned over her, so close she could feel the heat from his fit body as he insinuated himself into her personal space.

"Jess?"

"I prefer–"

"Martin."

"Martin, it's Jess—"

"The pub, come on."

"It's only four and... I..."

"I'd like you to."

"Yes, thank you, but..."

He reached towards her, his hand snaking across to touch the loose hair that refused to stay in place.

He smiled.

Her heart pounded.

"I imagine there must be a woman underneath that cold surface."

"I have to... erm. The report needs... you know."

"Your loss."

Once her computer was back on, it took Jessica several attempts to correct the errant apostrophe and she knocked her desk tidy onto the floor before she managed it. And she shredded two of the new reports by mistake and had to reprint them.

She should have gone with him and been part of the team. Joined in. Met someone special.

But she had an evening with the girls planned.

And Mister Gillet... Martin was trying to worm his way into her affections and that was good, wasn't it?

Surely, he was a catch, wasn't he?

He was a rising star in the council, a go-getter, and rich and handsome, and she could probably chip some of those awkward corners off him or learn to like his little ways.

So, it was either the pub with work colleagues or the wine bar with friends – it wasn't much of a contest.

It was well after 5:30 p.m. – she was going to have to claim some of that flexi back – when she hurried out of the offices towards the top of New Street and Chamberlain Square. The gleaming new office blocks, One and Two, towered above and then there was the war memorial on Centenary Square before she was finally amongst the cafés and bars by the canal.

Her friends had started without her.

"Sorry, sorry," she said. "Martin... Mister Gillet insisted, the report, you know. Oh, yes, yes."

Hannah poured her a glass of Prosecco. "You should tell him where to go," she said.

"Or let him have his way with you," said Olivia.

"Olivia! It's not like that," Jessica insisted.

"We've ordered," said Fiona.

"Oh, should I... did you? For me?"

"It's tapas."

"Oh, thank you."

She spilt her fizz on the table and swept a fork onto the floor trying to mop it up.

"Jessica, leave it alone," Hannah said.

"Let me clean it up."

"You need to get laid," added Olivia.

"No, really, I just... difficult day at the office."

Hannah, Fiona, Felicity, Parveen, Olivia and Jessica had all met on a course or had worked together. Thursdays were their day for a meal out at the Brasshouse: Prosecco and shots, catching up and later in the evening screeching at the gossip.

"Shall we get a stripper for Fi's hen do?"

"What?"

"A man!"

It was a good way to wind down from a hard week coping with the likes of Martin Gillet, whose strong arms—

"Jessica?"

"Sorry? Miles away. Hannah?"

"Olivia and I are going on to a club."

"Oh, no, not me."

"Got a man to go to?" Parveen asked.

"No!"

"You might meet someone," Hannah said.

"No. I'm... no. Tired, that's all."

"Come to the singles' bar with me," Olivia said.

"Not for me, thanks."

"You're not going to get a boyfriend, unless you take some risks," Olivia said. "Longing looks only go so far."

"Just an early night, thanks."

"Come on."

"It's only Thursday, I need to be at work tomorrow."

"If you fancy your boss, then do something about it."

"I'd rather not."

"Then move on to someone else."

"I'll think about it."

They said their goodbyes on the towpath, air kissing. Hannah, Felicity and Fiona went one way up the steps towards Broad Street, Parveen went along the edge of the canal one way and Olivia headed off in the other direction to go through the tunnel.

It was night already.

Jessica hurried after Olivia, not wanting to be alone.

The lights reflected off the dark water that rippled like oil. Lads laughed on a narrowboat, a stag party perhaps, or more likely bankers, roaring as they navigated the tunnel. Olivia's high heels echoed too under the brick arches as she negotiated the path. A couple on the bank opposite embraced, looking as if they were devouring each other's faces.

Jessica looked away.

Martin had a strong mouth and...

She hurried after her friend: Olivia would save her from these thoughts.

Perhaps she should even go with Oliva to the singles bar, just for a drink, a lemonade perhaps; at least see Olivia safely along the canal and into the club. She wouldn't go herself, of course, the place would be full of sharks.

"Olivia!"

Jessica hastened along the towpath that edged under the bridge, leaning to the left to avoid the curved ceiling.

Olivia was nowhere to be seen.

The bank opened out by the Tap and Spile as the canal widened into the Gas Street Basin. She wasn't there. She couldn't have made it to the pub entrance, could she?

Jessica looked about, feeling helpless.

"Olivia," she said, pointlessly.

She couldn't have missed her.

Jessica scooted further along, slipped and nearly fell on the wet surface where, somehow, the canal water had sloshed across the brick pavement.

A black and white iron bridge wasn't far away, reflected in the dark, still water, but Olivia wouldn't have crossed there. It only led to an artificial island built for narrow boats to tie up.

Couples came out of the next bar along to sit out by the canal and enjoy the cool breeze. She could see all the way along to the Mailbox with its bars and restaurants. No-one was walking that way.

Olivia had simply vanished.

♦

None of them saw Olivia that weekend – she'd scored!

Except, Jessica thought, she hadn't been into work on Friday. Perhaps she'd found someone, they'd said, which was why she wasn't picking up and texts remained unanswered.

By Monday morning, she'd plucked up the courage to knock on Mister Gillet's door.

"Mister—"

"Martin please, Jess."

"Sorry. And it's Jessica."

"I'll be with you in a moment, Jess," he said, going back to his computer screen.

Jessica looked out of his window down upon the city. Mister Gillet's office was high up, important, to reflect his rising status in the city. From here, she could look down upon the shops, offices and the expanse of wasteland, earmarked for development. There was a canal, quaint and picturesque, dividing the view. A narrowboat negotiated its way through the locks, the holidaymakers en route for the not-so-distant countryside. They turned the handles, the wooden gates opened and water gushed through into the lock, causing their boat to rise gradually to a new level.

"Well, Jess," said Gillett looking over.

Jessica pulled her attention back into the office: "It's... what did you say about disappearances?"

"There are no disappearances."

"It's my friend... Olivia. I've not heard from her since Thursday."

"She's probably gone off with someone," Martin said. "Do you fancy–"

"I'm worried."

He sighed: "When and where did you see her last?"

"Thursday night, she was going to a singles' bar."

"She wouldn't be single if she met me. Is she attractive?"

"Look please, she was going along the canal–"

"Canal!?"

"Yes."

"It's nothing, nothing at all. She probably met someone."

"Yes. Probably."

"Lots of bars along there, plenty of opportunities. So, let's just keep this quiet, shall we?"

"Well..."

"And when she gets in touch, just ask her who she was with all weekend."

He smiled, salaciously, his teeth orthodontically perfect and Jessica smiled too.

♦

Without knowing why, at lunchtime, instead of doing the site visit, Jessica found herself by the canal staring down into the deep water from the bridge.

Olivia still hadn't answered her phone.

There was a narrow staircase leading down to the canal.

Jessica jumped when some lads went past and shouted; they'd been drinking.

She kept close against the buildings as she went along the towpath.

Where to start?

She could ask in the bars, but the staff on now were most likely a different shift from the evenings. It was hopeless.

She'd gone back and forth a few times, tracing the route she'd taken only four days ago, before she became aware that she was being watched.

An old man sat on a narrowboat smoking a thin cigarette. His face was leathery, testament to years of living, and his fingers were stained with nicotine.

"Excuse me?"

He took his time: "I wondered when yow'd ask."

"Wondered?"

"Jarvis's the name."

"I'm Miss Bronson."

"Yow lookin' for someone?"

"Olivia," Jessica admitted.

"Disappeared?"

"Yes."

"Not the first, won't be the last."

"You saw something?"

"Not saw, exactly, but I know."

"Have you told the police?"

"Thay ayn interested."

"Why?"

He pointed: "Them's to blame."

Jessica could see the tunnel leading back to the restaurants along the canal, but she couldn't see who he meant. "I'm sorry."

"Yoewer Sea Life Centre."

"The Sea Life Centre?"

"Them do experiments, strange creatures, not natural," he said. "I've been on the water my whole life – navy, merchant navy, coastal boats and now the Babs."

Jessica glanced along the boat, the filigree painted sides and the legend '*Barbara*'.

"I've seen a lot of things," the man said. "I cud tell yow a few things and I know what's what about fish."

"Yes?"

"And there's summat in the water."

"Yes, fluoride for your teeth."

"Not tap water, yer numpty, the canal."

"Well, yes, you'd need your stomach pumped if you fell in and swallowed anything."

"I don't think yow'd get out. Fall in and yow'd be jedded for sure. Like I said, there's summat in the water. Summat alive. Summat real haiver."

"Haiver?"

"Big," he said, holding his hands far apart like a boasting fisherman.

Jessica didn't want to walk back along the bank – it was ridiculous, something in the water – but instead she nipped up the brick ramp and through an arch to Gas Street. Along the road and across Broad Street, she skirted the Brasshouse pub and effectively took the 'high road' pedestrian route by the restaurants a storey above the canal towpath.

The Sea Life Centre's modern façade overlooked a fork in the canal. In the centre of the waterway junction, there was an island, perhaps 6 or 7 metres in diameter with an old-fashioned signpost pointing to Worcester and Wolverhampton. Jessica chuckled: a circular railing protected the sign – an absurd indulgence given the surrounding wide moat of water.

Inside the Centre, it was a tropical paradise of palm trees, rocks and a waterfall. This is what an island should look like, Jessica thought: imagine being on a tropical island with a strong man in tight swimming trunks...

Opposite the sunny paradise, a cold Arctic scene dominated the flat wall. Jessica stared at it to cool down.

A sign asked her to '*start your dive here*'.

"Hello, hello, I'm Jessica Bronson with the Tourist Office."

She fished out her identity card, which the receptionist examined dubiously.

"I thought they closed."

"Just the Information Offices."

"No point having a Tourist Office if you don't give out the information, is there? Can I help you?"

Jessica had no idea why she was there.

"Er... I'd like to see someone about... what you do here?"

The receptionist grimaced: "There's Doug."

"Doug?"

"He's a marine biologist."

"He sounds perfect."

The receptionist nodded and disappeared through a door in the painted Arctic mural.

Penguins and palm trees – madness.

Doug was a pleasant, harmless looking man with glasses. "Hello, I'm Doctor Beale."

"Jessica Bronson, Tourist Information."

They shook hands. "How can I help you?"

"I wondered if you'd just explain what you do here."

"It's all on the website. We're one of a number of Sea Life Centres around the UK, but I think Birmingham's is the only sensible one in the country."

"Really?"

"Well, yes, the others, Great Yarmouth, Plymouth and so on are all by the sea. What's the point of going indoors when the sea is just next door?"

"Why indeed."

"Do you have any specific questions in mind?"

"I just wondered whether any creature has, you know, escaped from the Centre?"

"Escaped? To where? We're in the middle of the country. The sea is more than a hundred miles away."

"Into the canal," Jessica said pointing to the grim light in the opposite direction to the tropical scene. "We've more canals than Venice."

It sounded ludicrous now she'd said it out loud.

"Like what?"

"A shark?" *Oh, it was ludicrous.*

"Freshwater, not salt," Beale said, "it wouldn't survive."

Yes, completely ludicrous.

"It's just that there have been reports of something in the water and..."

"Something in the canal," he said. "There's tench, roach... carp, I guess."

"Something that can, you know... can they? Attack people?"

"No."

"Sorry. Of course. Thank you. Sorry to have taken up your time."

Jessica couldn't get out fast enough.

He'd been nice and she'd been stupid.

She rushed down the canal towpath as quickly as she could, upset at her own foolishness, and so she nearly collided with the policeman keeping people back.

It was a crime scene. She'd seen them on television and in films, and on photographs that required a statement that Birmingham was a safe tourist destination: such shocking incidents were thankfully extremely rare.

They had a boat and they were fishing some litter out of the canal, a fish or a piece of litter, jetsam washed up, something...

It was a human arm, its hand lolling... waving... beckoning...

There were spectators gawping everywhere, their arms raised to take photos – had they no respect?

Jessica staggered away, found the edge and threw up into the canal.

The mess spread out across the black surface.

The water moved, fish investigating the bounty.

Jessica wiped her mouth, found a tissue in her bag.

Someone muttered under their breath nearby: "Disgusting."

They meant Jessica: another silly girl drunk and it was only early afternoon on a Monday.

When Jessica glanced back again – she tried not to – the police were putting black bags into plastic storage boxes like so much rubbish.

And the crowd stared in mute fascination, some open-mouthed, some with glee and most through the screens of their phones.

Except one.

One face stared directly at her: Doctor Beale.

◆

The Hen Party had been postponed: no-one was in the mood for jolly japes once they heard the news about poor Olivia.

A few of them met on Thursday as usual, but they drank silently, made their excuses and left early.

"We should have got her a phone," Hannah said as she was leaving. "There's a whole batch of new smartphones coming in. There are apps to use if you're attacked."

Jessica answered: "She had a phone."

"Yes."

Jessica found herself alone with the meal she'd ordered, but couldn't stomach.

Poor Olivia.

Jessica decided she would live a little – follow Olivia's example – grab her chances when she could and not just sit here alone.

Oh God, someone might think she was single.

She was single.

There was nothing for her here, just a few sad old drunks and a weird writers' group meeting by the big window. She should go home, but then there was nothing for her in her apartment. There was no cleaning or tidying to do, nothing to take her mind off things. Even the dishwasher would have finished by now. Perhaps, she thought, she should get a cat.

"Miss Bronson?"

She jumped: it was Beale looking down on her like a predator, his glasses catching the light and making his eyes as dead as a shark's.

Uninvited, he sat opposite her: "I wanted to talk to you."

"I have to go," Jessica said.

Beale leant forward, moving the box of condiments out of the way so there was nothing protecting her from what he had to say.

"The body–"

"Please, don't–"

"I'm sorry, but the police–"

"She was killed."

"Not by a person," he said, excited. "I saw the wounds. They were bite marks."

"Please, no."

"I've studied marine predation. Your friend was killed by some sort of animal."

Jessica pushed away her gammon and chips, the plate splattered with ketchup and half-dissected meat.

"The police said–"

"The police don't know what they're talking about. I waited two hours to talk to Inspector Trent, but he wouldn't listen. Some incident at the Bull Ring is apparently more important."

Beale's tone reeked of anger, full of passion and now she looked at him again, he was quite attractive in a–

"I have to go," Jessica said.

"You talked about something in the water."

"Yes."

"What did you mean by that?"

"A man who lives on a boat said... and Olivia was walking by the canal when she disappeared. I was there, just behind her. I didn't see, but she can't have gone anywhere, no-one could have pushed her, there was no-one nearby. She was in high heels and had had a few drinks, but she wasn't that unsteady."

"So that only leaves...?"

"Something in the water."

♦

The next day Jessica took Beale to see the boatman Jarvis, who looked like he hadn't moved since she'd last talked to him. This would be the end of it, she thought. She'd introduce them and then go home to mug of hot chocolate with a shot of gin followed by a hot bath.

"Mister Jarvis, this is Doctor Beale."

"Ow bi'st gooin?"

"We'd like to hire your boat," Beale said.

Since when were they '*we*', Jessica wondered.

"Tha'll be fifty quid."

"You told my colleague that there was something in the water."

Since when were they '*colleagues*'?

"Damn roight, summat in the water."

"We'd like to catch it."

"Tricky."

"Will you help?"

"And who might yow be?"

"I'm Doctor Douglas Beale, a marine biologist at the Sea Life Centre."

"Yow be wantin' to catch one of yows freakish experiments."

"I assure you, we don't do anything of the sort."

"So yow say."

"So I say."

"Mister Jarvis, please," Jessica said. "Will you help us?"

"Aye, arm the only one on this cut who could. It'll still be fifty quid for yow and yow partner."

Since when were they '*partners*'?

"Doctor Beale isn't my partner," she insisted.

The old man glanced to one and then the other: "Yow look like a couple."

"We're not," Jessica insisted.

"If yow say so."

Beale interrupted: "About this creature?"

"Best when it's dark if yow want to see it."

"You've seen it? What was it?"

"A dark shape in the water."

"Can you show us?"

"Oilright, come aboard, I'll mek us sum tea."

"The *Barbara*, eh?" Beale asked.

"Second wife."

The inside of the narrowboat was filthy, smelt of diesel and his tea tasted disgusting. As the man chugged the boat along, Jessica sat below trying not to touch anything.

Dusk settled.

The lights of the city, distant from where they'd moored, lit up the sky, modern and inviting giving the gleaming metropolis a futuristic appearance. She could just about see the Rotunda, St Martin's spire and the sheen of the Selfridges building, all feminine curves and science fiction.

And she was in a grotty boat.

"It's toim," Jarvis announced.

Jessica came up on deck, finding it nearly impossible in the close confines at the back to stand without being uncomfortably close to Jarvis or, worse, Beale.

"Yow go fore," said Jarvis, "Miss Jessica."

"I beg your pardon."

"Yam lookout."

"Doctor Beale can do it."

"I need to get my kit ready in case," Beale said.

Jessica looked at the tangle of rods and nets that Beale had brought with him. He selected a strong pole and a particularly sturdy net.

"Arl be steerin' me boat," Jarvis replied. "Arl werk from this end by the lock and drive it to the far end. If yam lucky, and it's not in the loop, yam moight see it."

"Miss Bronson, if you do see something, shout out," Beale added, helpfully.

Jessica made her way along the thin and precarious walkway, nearly slipped a dozen times, until she came to the triangle of deck at the front. There was a door – she could have gone through the cabin instead of risking her life on the cliff's edge around the boat.

They set off.

Slowly.

People on the bank waved.

The first tunnel nearly freaked her out completely. The sound of the engine throbbed as the old, crumbling brick bounced the echo around in the coal dark.

The orange night sky finally reappeared above.

She felt she could breathe again.

Jessica gazed into the dark water, mesmerising by the bright lights reflecting on the oily surface. It was beguiling, despite everything. The surface of the canal was utterly calm ahead and then savagely cut into churning froth by the prow of the *Barbara*.

She found herself staring down at the bulge where the water rose before breaking, where the still water tried so hard to hold it together. Like her life really, constantly about to break into pieces.

She looked forward, away from such notions.

The dark canal was hypnotic, like a black motorway on a rain swept night. Colours smeared by the oily surface, the light catching the ripples to create a line of warning chevrons telling her to slow down.

Wait!

Something... but there was nothing, unless it was invisible or beneath the water creating the wake.

"There!" she shouted.

Beale stood on the top of the cabin: "Where?"

Jessica pointed desperately, and when she looked back–

Something broke the surface: teeth, snarling, eyes–

She shrieked like a hen party on Broad Street.

Jarvis slewed the boat hard round cutting the distance between them and the concrete bank, threatening to squash it in the narrowing gap.

Filthy water sprayed over the bow of the boat and droplets of filth splattered her fine suit.

The engine note rose.

The darkness in the black water snaked away.

They gave chase.

The *Barbara* turned out to be more speedboat than narrowboat.

"This is faster than regulation!" Jessica shouted.

Jarvis turned to Beale and grinned: Beale smirked back.

Men!

Maniacs.

At this souped-up speed, the swanky restaurants fell away, to be replaced by the derelict carcases of long forgotten factories.

"Yow gerrit! Yow gerrit!" Jarvis yelled.

Beale reached for his kit.

Jessica looked ahead: there was a bridge and under that was a lock. It was boxed in.

They'd trapped it.

Beale struggled with his flimsy pole and inadequate net.

The thing turned, coming towards them, a long bulge squirming powerfully and breaking the surface. It went to her right.

"Starboard side!" Jarvis hollered.

Beale shifted over.

"Yow other starboard!"

The thing powered beside the boat.

Jarvis pulled the tiller hard over and the boat caught the monster in a vice.

Its head broke the surface, screeching.

The boat lurched, pushed away by the thick bulk of the creature.

Jessica fell forward.

There was nothing to grab hold of, so she tumbled forward, the churning black water ready to swallow her. She slapped her hands against the bank, the stone sandpapering her palms as she slid until she was a bridge, held up by her feet in the boat and her hands on the towpath.

She saw the long length of the creature slithering through the gap.

The boat shifted away dragging her hand across the rough ground as the wooden edge skinned her shins.

Her ankles caught, her palms slid off the stone, her nails scraping and breaking.

From the water, teeth came up at her, sharp points!

A net caught the monster.

An arm around her waist, warm and pulling her close.

The thing yanked the net's pole free and swiped it back and forth as it tried to free itself.

Jessica fell into the deck on top of Beale.

"Did you see it?" he said, excited. "Magnificent."

Jessica struggled out of his clutches.

"It got away," Beale said. "I had to... save you."

Jarvis shouted from the rear of the boat.

Jessica didn't hear, her ears pounded and her lungs gulped air as she panicked.

Beale grabbed a pole and pushed against the bank, helping to turn the boat.

"Jarvis! It got past," he shouted. "We're going to need a wider narrowboat."

"Nonsense."

"It was an eel or a sea snake or... but gigantic. I don't know. Fabulous find."

"Yow sayin' it ain't one of yows monsters!"

"Not ours!"

It got past, Jessica realised. She scanned the canal, seeing the dark ribbon leading back to the city. It could be anywhere and there were all those people just wandering along the towpath just like Olivia.

Just as Jessica had herself.

Far away, a wooden rod jerked upright, quivering, and then it flattened again, away from them, which meant... she couldn't tell. There were ripples, a wake far greater than such a flimsy pole should create, but at this distance, was it coming towards them or going away?

Ominously, it submerged beneath the water.

Even the net's pole had gone.

The ripples subsided and the dreadful calm settled.

Whatever it was, marine experiment or freak of nature, it was gone. Slunk away for easier prey perhaps... prey like Olivia.

A shape appeared like a rising periscope, a rod made of wood.

"B..." Jessica couldn't get her throat to work, she couldn't breathe, she couldn't move...

The boat jolted, rose and she nearly fell from the port side. The pole snapped up, flicking dirty water in a line across them.

Beale caught it, held on, but it tugged him outwards.

It was Jessica's turn to grab hold of him.

"Thanks, I—"

The pole came loose – no net!

The boat juddered again.

Splintering wood cracked below.

The *Barbara* slewed sideways, pushed as powerfully crabwise through the water as the engine could drive it forward.

Then it juddered, bouncing up and down.

"Gone under us!" Jarvis yelled. "Babs is takin' in water."

The calm surface before the lock exploded upwards like a geyser.

"It's going for another run at us," Beale shouted. "Get back to the Sea Life Centre!"

"Arl try."

The engine chugged as Beale pushed at the bank again, turning them, just not quickly enough. The prow crashed into the stonework, scraped along and then the vessel leapt forward, picking up speed.

Their passage back took them between the abandoned factories and, too far ahead, the bright lights of the city beckoned, the neon and dazzle turning disturbingly as if the view was mocking them. Everything slanted, the horizon untrue.

The boat was listing!

And the water threatened to flow over the edge.

"Doctor Beale!" Jessica said, glancing into the cabin. Pots and pans floated between the cupboards.

"Miss Bronson?"

"We're sinking!"

"More speed!" Beale shouted sternwards.

"I imagine he's put his foot down!" Jessica screeched.

She checked the stern, saw the grim determination on the weathered face of their captain as he manned the tiller. Behind him, a black shape weaved and danced, eyes catching the light, and then it swooped down, its mouth going around the man and lifting him bodily out of the boat.

Jessica screamed.

For a moment, Jarvis's legs flailed upwards in the air and then he disappeared into the water.

There was an appalling gap where Jarvis had been, the tiller unmanned and the desperate engine still racketing on. The canal side seemed to smear sideways as the boat turned.

Beale went aft, trying to move as fast as possible along the narrow walkway back to the controls.

Jessica saw a pub, its warm, inviting glow—

The boat smashed into something. Jessica fell as the water in the cabin sloshed forwards, drenching her. The boat lifted upwards, the broken deck inside threatening to become a wall.

It exploded.

The narrow, streamlined face of the monster penetrated the planking and the thing slithered through the bilge towards her. Its gills pulsated sickeningly at the side of its head as its engorged length writhed and squirmed. The long, powerful body forced itself through the crack along with the gushing water.

She grabbed the nearest weapon at hand, a fire extinguisher attached to the wall, but it stuck fast. The creature sensed her weakness and arched its sinuous neck preparing to attack.

Jessica yanked and the wood split as the extinguisher and its mounting bracket came free. It was heavy, but she whirled round and used it as a blunt instrument.

The monster jerked back, hissed loudly and coiled ready to strike once more.

She hit it again, and fell backwards out of the cabin back onto the foredeck.

The filthy bilge water splashed about her as she half-scrabbled, half-swam backwards to the point of the bow. She kept the fire extinguisher between her and the creature, but the weight slowed her down, threatened to pin her underwater.

She was trapped, the thing was almost upon her.

"Jump off!" It was Beale, shouting. "Save yourself."

"What about—"

The creature struck again., its mouth wrapping around the fire extinguisher as it tried to tear her protection away.

Jessica struggled; the cylinder came free leaving the creature to bend and crunch the metal bracket in its jaws.

Where was Beale?

She had to save him.

He had to save her!

There was a brick floor behind her... getting further away as the gap grew.

What about Beale?

She couldn't leave him, but she couldn't see him.

It was either jump or stay in the boat – no other choice.

Jessica clambered onto the edge and launched herself into space. For a moment, she was airborne, flying, and then she landed hard, pitched forward and crashed into an iron railing.

The fire extinguisher, spat towards her like a bullet, sounded a metallic note as it bent the metalwork.

The thing came for her like a snake shedding the skin of the wooden boat. Before its tail had left the doomed vessel, it had plunged into the water only to re-emerge, springing upwards to splash onto the ground.

Side-winding on the narrow path, it hunted Jessica.

She escaped along a tightly curved railing, going round and back on herself in a circle. The land was round, only a few metres in diameter – she was on the island!

And there was nowhere to go.

It was only a step further to reach the creature's pulsating body as it constricted and bent the iron railing. Its head closed in behind her, jaws snapping.

Jessica turned, pulled the pin from the fire extinguisher and squeezed the handle together. The weapon fired, white gas exploding outwards and enveloping the monster.

She kept hold of the cold spray, seeing a dark shape writhe in the fog.

Then the CO_2 ran out.

She threw the spent metal canister and saw it bounce off something looming out of the mist.

A splash!

Jessica vaulted the railing into the nettles.

She grabbed the signpost in the centre, leapt up to grasp the metal pointers. Left hand on 'British Waterways Visitor Information Centre and Gift Shop 200 yds', right hand on 'Wolverhampton 13 miles 3 locks' and left hand up again to 'Fazeley 15 miles 38 locks'.

Terror gave her strength to climb further and pull herself up by the round 'Old Turn Junction' at the top, her heeled shoes catching the lower rung now and propelling her to the summit, her haste threatening to pitch her over the other side.

All around there was white mist, a veil hiding everything, and then the cold dispersed, filtering away to reveal first the railing below, the tiny brick island and finally the ominously calm dark water of the canal.

♦

A group of lads going along the bank pointed and laughed. They must have thought she'd been dumped there as part of some hen night prank or something.

Jessica tried to manoeuvre downwards but found it difficult. Her limbs seemed to have a mind of their own, some strong primate instinct, for they refused to let go of the metal tree she'd climbed.

Finally, Douglas Beale arrived in a narrowboat, a floating café, and it took him and two others to coax her down. It was frightening to step back onto a boat and surreal to walk between the tables and chairs in the cabin.

The diners continued to eat their cake and drink their tea.

Jessica shook uncontrollably.

When they reached the shore, she practically flew out onto the hard, dry land.

It was a while before she could speak: "Did we... is it?"

He shook his head.

♦

"Look," Gillet said, "if there is a creature, and I'm not saying there is, then it's clearly trapped in a small section of the canal system and—"

He was an ugly man, Jessica decided, not outside, but under his smooth surface.

"A small section with all the canalside restaurants," Jessica said, staggered that he didn't understand the danger.

"We looked, it's gone."

"Mister Gillet—"

"Martin, please. Jess."

"It's Miss Bronson."

"Excuse me, but your tone isn't appropriate," Gillet said. "I am your line manager."

"And as such responsible for any further deaths."

"I think not. It's not my department."

"Really!?"

"If you are going to make trouble, perhaps you should consider your position here."

Jessica looked down.

The city was below, a tapestry of loose threads and areas of colour. There was a surprising amount of green in Birmingham.

A canal, a dark line of water, cut across far below the window. It was sub-divided by the two gates of a lock. As she watched, the water seemed to rise as a thick, black line snaked outwards and looped around the first gate. It didn't seem to move, but then the tail flicked and the creature repeated the action around the next gate leaving a curve of damp ground to show its passage. Its route was back towards the bright lights, bars and restaurants, fancy shops and future hopes.

"Yes," she said. "It's time to move on."

In the street, after she'd handed back her pass to the surprised security guard, Douglas Beale was waiting for her.

"Well?"

"He's an idiot!"

"Same in my department," Beale said. "The find of a lifetime, but not if affects visitor numbers."

"Doctor Beale, I'm sorry."

"Douglas."

"Sorry?"

"I'm Douglas."

"Jessica."

"Jessica," he said and she liked the sound of her name on his lips. "If you'll risk it, would you like to, you know, go out for a meal? Together, I mean?"

Jessica thought about it: "Nowhere near a canal please."

"We could go to New Street, find somewhere nearby or even catch a tram somewhere?"

"I'd like that," Jessica said. "You know, we've 21 kilometres of tram. Venice only has 19 kilometres."

"Really?"

"Oh yes, Birmingham has more tramlines than Venice."

---

*David Wake is an eclectic writer of science fiction (*1, Phone *and the* Thinkersphere *series), steampunk (*The Derring-Do Club *series) and politics (*Crossing the Bridge*). With Andy Conway, he published the non-fiction book* Punk Publishing *(see:* **punkpublishing.co.uk***) as a definitive guide to why and exactly how to publish independently. He invented the literary form of the Drabble. Join his mailing list at* **davidwake.com.**

Meet Me on the Corner

David Muir

"You've had the dream again, I can tell?"

I nodded. "Sorry if I've been quiet today."

My wife held my arm. "You're too hard on yourself, dear. I'll meet you up there later."

New Street had altered beyond recognition since the end of the war. Sixty years since I waited near Victoria Square, an event that echoes down the decades.

I walked slowly to the corner at the top of the street and let my memory unfold.

♦

Bullets zipped and fizzed over our heads, forcing us to remain crouched in a perilous position. Our orders were to push on towards the centre of Caen by following the line of the canal, but heavy rifle and machine gun fire kept us pinned down behind a low wall.

"We've got to get out of here," yelled Captain Roberts over the din that raged around us.

Pretty bloody obvious.

Another shower of brick fragments rained down on us. Fear etched on dusty faces. Silent glances exchanged. I could hear the alarm in our captain's voice. He was younger than the rest of us. I didn't blame him: we were all scared.

"The mortars are getting closer," he shouted.

Another blindingly inescapable observation.

We were powerless as long as we remained trapped behind the wall.

"Let's see if we can make it back to the houses," bellowed Corporal Styles. "We can't just sit here."

"We go two at a time," shouted the Captain. "Styles and Jones go last just before me. Let's get out of here."

Bradfield and Marshall set off the way we had come, running low, weaving from left to right through smoke and dust until they were lost from sight. The rest retreated in pairs until three of us remained.

Styles and I looked at one another, nodded and ran.

A shell smacked into the ground to my left and exploded with a heavy crump. Shrapnel tore the air. Something hit my left thigh as I flung myself forward. I reached down instinctively, felt my trousers all sticky, collapsed and tried to get to my feet. Shells detonated on all sides, obscuring my vision. The uproar grew louder. I tried to get up again but fell face first.

"Styles, are you all right?" I cried as another shell burst, sending deadly fragments in all directions.

Styles was pulling me backwards, carrying my helmet and our rifles. I couldn't see much of him from my prone position as he grunted and dragged me towards where we thought the others were.

Captain Roberts dashed forward and they carried me between them. I hopped on my good leg, trying to help them.

The next shell brought us down. Roberts took the full force of it. Styles threw himself on top of me, then hauled me to safety behind the end house.

I asked Styles if he was all right.

He slumped against what remained of the back wall of the house. "We best get out of here," he said.

"Just another minute," I croaked.

I saw him raise a hand weakly, thumb in the air, before I passed out.

♦

I remember little about being transferred from Caen: stretchers, field hospitals and faces. Kind faces, worried faces looking down at me as I lay helpless, fearful of the extent of my injuries. I bounced around in an ambulance, drifting in and out of consciousness; a rough ferry crossing; a train to London.

The hospital was fully prepared for our arrival. Nurses and doctors milled around the fleet of ambulances that disgorged wounded men; some walking, others, like myself, unable to. My neck ached from several days of looking up either at the sky or the roof of an ambulance. I longed to see the horizontal world again.

Arriving at St Thomas's came as a huge relief after my arduous passage from the war zone to what I hoped would be the peace and calm of England. The battle for Caen had been ferocious. There were faces of brave pals I would never see again, lost in the campaign to liberate France. I'd been lucky to come out alive. Even the severe pain in my leg seemed to recede as they took me inside, removed my filthy uniform, changed my dressings and lowered me onto a bed. A nurse stuffed pillows behind my back and raised me so I could see my surroundings.

"Thank you, nurse," I said as she made me comfortable. "It's good to sit up at long last."

"One of the doctors will see you soon," she said. "Your wounds aren't so serious, so it might be a while before we get to you."

"That's all right. I'm just so glad to be here."

Our ward contained men who hadn't been badly wounded; the really grave cases must be elsewhere. I got a lot of sleep and they cleaned and dressed my leg wounds several times.

I asked one of the doctors about my injuries.

"We couldn't find any shrapnel. Your field hospital did a good job on you. It's now a matter of seeing how well your leg heals."

"Thanks, Doc. Would someone have time to do something for me? I'd like to find out if a Corporal Sam Styles is here. We're in the same regiment, the Royal Warwickshire. I lost track of him after Caen."

"I'll see what I can do," he replied.

A few hours later, a nurse approached my bed. "Corporal Styles is in a ward at the other end of the corridor. He's asking after you."

"Thanks, nurse. Can I go and see him?"

"You're quite good on your crutches. I'll ask the doctor if we can let you." The nurse returned a few minutes later. "Doctor MacLeod says you can see him. Take it carefully though."

I swung myself out of bed, put on a dressing gown and hobbled along the ward to the usual chorus of ribaldry. My stomach knotted during the several minutes it took me to reach Sam's ward. Questions about his injuries tumbled around my head. I shouldered my way through the double doors and looked along the rows of beds. I found Sam in the third on the left.

"Hello, mate. How're you doin'?" he asked weakly.

"Not too bad. It's good to see you. We made it then."

"More than you can say about the captain. There wasn't much left of him, was there?"

"He took the full brunt of it. Where'd you get hit?"

"Stomach and side, all down here," Sam pointed. "Pretty bad. How about you?"

"Lots of shrapnel in my left leg. They got it all out, though."

"And you can walk okay?"

"With an effort. Between the two of you, you saved my life. I never got the chance to thank you."

"You'd have done the same."

"How you found the strength to drag me all that way, I'll never know."

"You're a big bloke and what with all your kit..."

"I can't find the words to thank you enough, Sam."

31

"'S'all right, mate. We both made it home, that's the main thing."

I visited Sam most days during the weeks that followed. We rabbited on about how glad we were to be out of the war. We talked about our families and where we lived on opposite sides of Birmingham.

"Have you got a photo of your family?" I asked Sam one day.

"In the drawer there. I can't reach it."

"In here?" I handed Sam his battered wallet.

"That's my missus and our boy. He's a few years older now."

A dark-haired woman holding the hand of a small boy smiled from a creased and blurred photograph.

"You'll see 'em soon, Sam."

"Who have you got to go home to?" asked Sam.

"Just me and my mum. Hope she hasn't rented out my room."

"Ooh, don't make me laugh, mate. It hurts."

I put Sam's wallet back in the drawer. "See you soon. I'd better get back to my ward."

My next visit to Sam turned out to be my last. We were chatting about Birmingham pubs.

"I drink at the Bull in Stechford. What's your local?" asked Sam.

"The Plough and Harrow in Selly Oak, near where I live with my mum. Listen, Sam, they're sending me home in a day or two. Do you know when you'll be out of here?"

"Dunno, mate. I reckon I could be here for a while."

"Let's meet for a pint when we get home."

"Good idea. When and where?"

"What about Christmas Eve? We'll remember that. In the city centre," I suggested. "If your wife and kid won't mind."

"That's far enough ahead. I'll be back on my feet by then."

"Let's say midday, at the top of New Street, Galloways Corner. We could have a pint or two, then go home to our families in plenty of time for Christmas Eve proper."

We shook on it and I returned to my ward.

♦

I could walk with the aid of a stick and my wounds had healed sufficiently for me to leave St Thomas's. My regiment relieved me from any further war duties and I was officially demobbed in October. I spent the next month at my grandmother's house, going for walks along the coast of Devon until I gained enough strength to walk without a stick. The battle for Caen left me with a limp and my leg ached from time to time: a small price to pay for my survival.

After a few weeks of sea air, I went home to my mum's council house. She encouraged me to find out if I could get my old job back at the tram depot in Selly Oak. Old Bert, the foreman, said he would let me know. Most of the mechanics' jobs had gone to women while the men had enlisted. For the time being, I was out of work and living off my mum and felt a bit guilty getting a Blighty. Bert and the other blokes at the depot treated me with respect though, something which made me feel welcome to be home.

As Christmas approached, I thought about Sam. We hadn't got round to exchanging addresses, but I doubted that either of us were letter-writing types.

I made sure I was early and waited near the entrance to Galloways camera shop on the corner of New Street, keeping a lookout for Sam. Shoppers bustled past me, intent to make the best of Christmas despite the continuing war in Europe. Anticipation turned into disappointment as the minutes ticked past twelve o'clock. Perhaps dragging me out of there was not as significant to Sam as it was to me: he said he was only doing his duty, just like anyone else. For all I knew, he simply didn't want to be reminded about what had happened.

I was on the point of giving up when a boy approached me.

"Are you Mister Jones?"

"That's me," I said.

"My mum sent me. My dad can't come."

"Oh, that's a shame. I was..."

"My dad's dead."

Words formed in my head but made no sound. The shock of this matter-of-fact announcement left me staring at Sam's son.

"He wanted you to have this."

I took something from his outstretched hand. It took me a few seconds to realise I was holding our regimental cap badge.

Sam's cap badge.

"Your dad was a very brave man, he saved my li–"

I looked up. The boy was gone, lost in the crowd of Christmas shoppers. I hobbled down New Street trying to find him in the throng. I crossed the busy street and looked up and down before re-crossing and returning to Galloways Corner. I searched until my wounded leg ached from dragging it in a frantic limp.

Dejected and distressed, I abandoned the search after jostling and bumping into several more people and took refuge on the corner of the Waterloo Bar, away from the crowds.

The boy was nowhere to be seen; it was a hopeless task. The antlers of the antelope emblem on Sam's cap badge had dug into my palm and drawn blood. I made for the flight of steps up to Waterloo Street, slumped on the bottom step and rubbed at the pain in my leg. My mind raced back to that afternoon in Caen when Corporal Sam Styles had pulled me away from certain death.

There was no one to help me this time.

♦

My wife waved as she approached. "Feeling better?"

"Better now," I lied, stifling the catch in my voice.

"Are you ready to go yet?"

"Just another minute."

Her arm around my waist steadied my shaking limbs. My throat tightened and I felt the familiar threat of tears forming.

We stood together and waited until the pull of the past let me go, until the next time the dream unspooled.

David Muir was born in Scotland in 1947 and attended a number of boarding schools in the Midlands area. After a spell trying to be a schoolteacher, he spent over twenty years as a lecturer in one of the new universities in the West Midlands, where he wrote a number of technical books on computing. Having now retired, he spends time writing fiction, a blog and poetry. He lives with his wife in Solihull. Find David at **davidmuir.org**.

MEANWHILE...

Silver Star and Pumpkin Girl

Tony Cooper

A "Powerless" short story

"Hey girl!"

Hayley spun round to see her old school friend Alice jogging towards her. She flung her arms wide and they hugged.

"You're looking good, Pumpkin," said Hayley.

"You too, Silver Star!" beamed Alice.

'Silver Star' was the Hero name that Hayley made up for herself as a child. She, Alice and another girl called Michelle, used to play in the woodland near their homes in Harborne. Alice was 'Pumpkin Girl', or 'The Raging Satsuma', on account of her bright ginger hair and nutritionally balanced lunchbox contents, and Michelle made up the group as 'The Grim Reaper', and loved hamming it up, until she reached the age when such things were beneath her, and their terrible trio became a dynamic duo instead.

Of course, none of Hayley's friends knew that she was a real hero. She'd discovered her powers of teleportation one day, whilst nearly falling to her death. Nowadays she was no longer 'Silver Star', but had her own real Hero name, and it was no longer for play.

"It's been *far* too long since I saw you last," Hayley said.

Alice swatted the air dismissively, "Don't worry about it, your life's way busier than mine. Oh, speaking of business... brought you something from my shop!" said Alice, pulling out from her bag a large plastic cup filled with an orangey liquid. "Carrot, sweet potato and kale smoothie, topped with acai berries, crushed almonds and granola."

Hayley gingerly took the cup, "That's amazing. I love how you've managed to combine everything I avoid eating in one handy container."

Alice laughed and soft-punched her in the stomach, "Perfect energiser and protein mix for someone with such a hectic life as you."

It had been many years since Hayley had returned to Birmingham to meet up with friends. Her job as a police constable in Element City took up most of her 'normal' time, and her life as the vigilante crime fighter 'Jump' took up the rest. Two lives, constantly competing for priority. It was tiring, for sure, but Hayley couldn't imagine it any other way.

As they walked down New Street from Victoria Square, Alice brought up the boyfriend question, as always. Hayley rolled her eyes, tried to change the subject, and even promised to drink Alice's concoction if she shut up about it, but she wasn't going to be defeated.

"You're not back with Gary from work, are you?" asked Alice.

"No way. Nobody from work."

"Ah! So there *is* someone!"

Hayley cursed silently, "You know, I think you'd make a great detective. Could you take my exams for me?"

"No dawdling – tell all!"

The only man in Hayley's life right now was Martin, an old Hero from the 90s – she'd saved his life. Twice. They had been working together as a Hero team for over a year now, and he was training her up.

"Well, I know this older guy, who's pretty cool. We meet up for coffee and chats, that sort of thing."

"Nice to have a coffee and a chat when you wake up in the morning..."

"Oh no, nothing like that! It's completely platonic. He's just helping me... find out a few things about myself."

Alice raised an eyebrow, "Yeah, that's what I was meaning."

"I see *you* haven't changed. *Aaa*-nyway, moving swiftly on, how's business? 'Super Smoothies', is it?"

"Yeah, I wanted to call it 'Superhero Smoothies', but the council objected. They're touchy about anything associating itself with Heroes, but I thought I'd give it a go. Anyhow, business is good. Just taken on another person, so that's two staff and myself now. Means I can steal away for a couple of hours to meet an old friend, which is handy!"

"Neat."

"And I see you're still holding that cup away from you like it's going to explode."

"Just judging how far I can walk before dumping it in a bin and causing the least amount of offence."

"Don't you dare."

"Speaking of old friends, you still in touch with 'The Grim Reaper'? How is she?"

For a moment, they both hesitated, as they remembered their old playmate.

"Yeah, good. Don't see Michelle as often now. She's still soliciting... I mean, being a solicitor! I did that joke on her once and it went down like a fart at a funeral."

"I can imagine."

"She's specialising now in Hero law or something. Taking on cases where someone was injured or killed by a Hero, making sure they're compensated properly."

Hayley thought of all the henchmen she'd knocked the teeth out of, and imagined them all sitting in a row outside Michelle's office, still clutching at their jaws.

Alice tugged at her arm and pointed towards a large store front, "That's my local Primark. I get my knickers from there. Dead cheap."

"Looks like a tornado has ripped through it."

"Yeah, it's always like that."

As Alice was speaking, Hayley spotted a man moving oddly through the crowd. Even though she tried, it was hard to turn off the 'police' in her. You would try to relax, but then your radar would ping. It wasn't just her, it was the same with her colleagues.

Alice was talking about Element City now, hoping she could come visit her one weekend, but Hayley's eyes were still on the man. He was small, about her height, but so wide across the shoulders his hoodie was stretched. It was the way he walked very carefully, avoiding getting near anyone, the way he looked around too.

Of course, everybody looked around when they were out shopping, but this was different – he kept glancing over towards store fronts, checking above the doors, presumably for security cameras. When they passed a CCTV camera on a traffic light pole, he bowed his head even lower.

She and Alice walked past the Rotunda, towards the entrance of the Bullring Shopping Centre. The man went the same way. He glanced over towards the building society on the corner and Hayley finally saw part of his face.

"So, I was thinking sometime in August maybe? I could stay overnight? We could watch crappy horror movies and stuff ourselves with organic chocolate!"

'Oh crap,' thought Hayley. The man was Frantic. He was the only inmate still on the run after last year's break-out from Woodhall, the high security prison for dangerous, powered criminals.

"I mean, I don't mind sleeping on the floor. Or we could share a bed, like when we had sleepovers! I'm only little, as long as you don't sleep like a starfish."

Hayley saw two police officers walking out from the Bullring. They were armed, and scanning the crowd, one of them pressing his finger into his ear.

"They've seen him."

"...said I snored like a walrus! What a cheek! I *know* I don't... what?"

One of the officers nudged the other and nodded over towards Frantic. He hadn't seen them yet, still busy checking the shop doorways for cameras. The officers made some space between themselves, and put their hands on their MP5 submachine guns.

"Oh God, not here. Just follow him on camera, track him from a distance and get him when he's away from the crowds. Don't try and be heroes."

"Who are you talking to Hayley? What's... what's going on."

"Something really bad."

One of the officers waved a family group out of the way and they both raised their weapons to the man in the hoodie as he walked past the bull statue.

"Frantic! Stop right there! Get on the ground now."

The man froze on the spot.

"Oh wow, who is that?" said Alice, as Hayley put a hand on her shoulder and edged them towards a shop window.

"Someone very bad."

An arena of gasping shoppers quickly formed around the stand-off.

"I said, get on the ground, NOW!"

Frantic looked side-to-side. The officers crept towards him. Hayley's heart leapt into her throat. "No, you fools, wait for backup!"

"Frantic, get your hands in the air!"

"On the ground!" said the other officer.

Frantic finally looked directly at the two officers, rifles pointed at him. He spoke carefully and slowly, "You don't look like PCA to me."

"The Powered Crime Agency are on their way, so you're going to sit tight until..."

"So... they're not here yet?"

The first officer hesitated slightly, "They're on their way and…"

"So, you've no backup, and you know bullets bounce off me? Don't you? You did read that part of my file?"

Neither officer said anything.

"You didn't?" continued Frantic "Oh, well now. Someone's just made a very bad call. And for once, it wasn't me."

"Cl… clear the area. Everybody clear the area immediately!"

Alice tip-toed to look between the heads of the crowd. "Who is it? Who have they caught?"

"No-one. Nobody is caught. That's the problem. Alice?"

"Yeah?"

Hayley pressed the smoothie cup into her hand, "Do me a favour and run."

"What?"

"Yep, like, *really* fast in the opposite direction."

"Why?"

The officers held their position. "I said clear the area! This man is powered. Everyone get out of here now!"

Some of the crowd took the hint, but the rest were far too interested to move, most hidden behind their mobile phones recording the scene.

Frantic slowly removed his hands from his pockets, took the rim of his jacket hood and pulled it down to reveal a mostly shaven head, with several, parallel mini-mohicans, all dyed flame red. "You want me officers? You got me!" he said, then ran at them.

"Alice, GO! NOW!" Hayley pushed her away, "Everybody get dow…"

Her shout was cut short by the snapping sounds of two submachine guns opening fire. Bullets bounced off Frantic's skin, ricocheting randomly into the crowd. Screams followed, *then* people ran.

One of the officers dropped to the floor, hit by a bullet. Frantic left-hooked the other and sent him flying. He slammed into the shop window next to Hayley, shattering it into a spider's web, and slumped to the ground.

"Who's next then?" shouted Frantic.

And Hayley knew there would be more. Frantic had a hair-trigger temper that would not go away until he was sure every last threat was gone. And right now, everybody taking videos and pictures of him was a threat.

As he lunged towards the back of the fleeing crowd, Hayley knew what she had to do. But first, she had to find somewhere safe to jump back to. Teleporting home for a quick change wasn't the problem, she had a safe area all cleared out, but teleporting back was dangerous. She couldn't just jump back to where she was standing; if someone was in that spot at the same time, it would end in a Cronenberg nightmare for them both.

Glancing around, there was only one safe spot. It was a bit public, but it would have to do. She ran, blending in with the crowd, then she jumped.

♦

By the time she got back, Frantic was stooping over three people lying on the ground, grinding their phones to powder with his heel, and about to do the same to their heads.

"Hey, Frantic!"

He turned to see a blonde-haired girl wearing a black leather jacket, purple Venetian mask and purple yoga pants (which happened to be on inside-out), standing on the Bullring Bull statue.

She smiled at him, "How about you get *my* number first?"

Frantic smiled back, nodding. He forgot about his prey on the ground. They scrambled to their feet and ran.

"Hell yeah! It's been far too long since I took down a Hero. Looks like this is my lucky day!"

There was still a large crowd gathered, although they were watching from a much safer distance. Or so they thought. Hayley knew how fast this big guy could move given enough space. She would have to try and either take him down fast and hard, or just teleport him far away from here so he couldn't hurt anybody. But both plans would mean getting within touching distance.

A third option was to keep him occupied long enough until the PCA arrived with their specialist anti-Hero equipment. How long that would take, she had no idea. And she had no idea if she had the energy to last that long.

Frantic ran towards her.

'No time like the present,' she thought, and leaped forward, arms stretched out.

She reappeared right next to Frantic. Wrapping her arm around his neck as if it was a pole, she swung around the back of him, pulling him over. He slammed into the ground, back of his head first, to a loud 'Ooh' from the crowd.

But Frantic quickly brought his hands up and grabbed her arm so hard she felt the bone squeal. She teleported away, leaving Frantic grasping at empty air. He flipped over onto his front, and looked around, snarling like a wild dog.

"Come back and fight, you..."

Hayley landed in the middle of his back, having jumped twenty feet above him, and letting gravity do the rest. Remembering his speed, she hopped away, just missing his grasp again as he swung his arm blindly behind him.

He got back onto his feet and faced her.

"I dunno who you are girl, but you're going to end up a red smear on the ground just like everyone else who's crossed me."

"You'll have to catch me first," she said, turning tail and running towards the bull statue.

She could hear Frantic's feet pounding close behind her. Almost on her. She leaped forward, bringing her right knee up... jumped behind him and buried her knee in the small of his back, sending him stumbling forwards and slamming face-first into the bull.

"It's always the same with you bodybuilding types. You do so much work on your arms and legs, but forget about your back. You should take up yoga, really work on those core muscles."

Then she spotted some of the crowd creeping forward, angling for a good picture. She had to get them back. She teleported as close to them as she dared, covering the exposed part of her face from the phone cameras.

"Get out of here now! This guy will kill you! Go on, bloody run!"

"Not if you're here!"

"Yeah, you're going to kick his arse!"

Sometimes Hayley forgot that the last time Heroes properly fought in public was back in the early nineties. Nobody had any idea of the real danger they were in.

A loud rending of metal made her look behind.

Frantic was wrenching the bull from the ground, concrete tumbling from its hooves. As he lifted it over his head he said, "Yeah. You'd bloody better run," then threw it.

The giant bull tumbled through the air, and over Hayley's head, in a surprisingly graceful arc towards the crowd. Some ran, some cowered, but most of them hadn't even realised what was happening yet. She only had seconds. Hayley quickly judged the arc of the bull, teleported onto a plant pot under its flightpath, and waited. She reached up her hand, bent her knees and prepared herself. This was going to take... perfect... timi...

Like a basketball player stretching every sinew for the ball flying over their head, she leapt. The crowds' scream turned into a gasp, as both she, and the bronzed bull, disappeared.

Suddenly, from the opposite direction came a large, metallic 'bang', followed by an "Ow!"

Those that turned their heads in time, just managed to see Frantic cracked across the back of his head, and sent sprawling across the ground by the bull, which landed on its feet and slid to a triumphant halt some distance away.

Frantic was out cold.

There was a cautious cry of joy from the crowd, followed by the insect clicking of camera phones as PCA officers arrived on the scene.

♦

Ten minutes later Alice finally found Hayley. She was checking on an elderly woman, who was sat against one of the large plant pots. The woman was having trouble breathing, and Hayley waved to get the attention of a paramedic. When she saw Alice, she stood up, wincing in pain as she clutched her right forearm, and walked over to her friend.

"Hayley, you okay?"

"Er... yeah, some idiot pushed me over as they ran away. Done something to my wrist."

"Come on, there's an ambulance over there."

Hayley shook her head, "No, no. It's nothing. Some people here got hit by bullets, they..."

"...are being taken care of already, so now it's time for *you* to get some help. Come on," she grabbed Hayley's other arm, "With me. I'm taking you over there..."

"No, Alice, I'm fine, I can..."

"Not hearing you! Gone deaf!"

Hayley didn't have the energy to complain. All that teleporting without a prior calorie binge had exhausted her completely, not to mention the walk back down from the toilets at New Street Station, the safest place she could think of teleporting back to blind.

When she returned to the Bullring, the PCA were taping off the crime scene. They had already arrested Frantic. He was still unconscious.

Moments later, Hayley and Alice were sat on the back step of an ambulance, Hayley with her right wrist tightly bandaged.

"Well," said Alice, "That made for an interesting break from work. Not what I'd planned for us."

"Yeah, your precognition powers suck."

Alice stuck her tongue out. "You know, playing superheroes in the woods was nothing like this. I think it's best to leave the heroics to the actual Heroes."

Hayley smiled, "Given I can't even walk twenty metres without breaking something, yeah, probably best."

"I wonder who that girl was. You think she's that one from Element City? The father and daughter team – the muscle and the teleporter?"

The 'father and daughter' team was a reference to Martin and herself. It was an assumption by the PCA which, handily, helped keep them from being properly identified. The cheap masks helped too.

"Well, she's a teleporter. She can be anywhere she wants, I guess."

Alice nodded. "Mmm, I suppose she's just like anyone else really. Probably has friends here, you know, pops over for a visit."

She turned the smoothie cup round in her hands as Hayley looked at her. Did she know?

Alice and Michelle had been in the woodland the day she teleported for the first time. All they saw was her leaping blindly off a hidden cliff, then when they ran home to tell her father, Hayley was already there. She thought she'd got away with it, saying she'd landed in a bush and found another way home, but had often wondered whether they suspected.

Michelle had surely worked it out, but had said nothing. It was soon after that she stopped meeting up with them. But Alice was the youngest of their group, only six at the time. She couldn't have worked it out, could she? Surely, she couldn't have known all this time and said nothing?

Alice gave a big beaming smile, "And I guess she saves a hell of a lot on train fares."

"Yeah, I... I guess so."

Alice shoved the smoothie cup into her face, "Now get this down your neck before you think up another excuse, Silver Star."

Hayley sighed as she took the cup and gingerly sipped through the straw, "You know, this isn't actually that bad."

Alice gently elbowed her in the ribs, "Energy boost," she smiled, "You got my back, I got yours. After all, what are best friends for, eh?"

Hayley smiled back, "I mean, I don't want to spew *quite* yet, but give me a minute."

"Moron."

They laughed, then sat together in silence, both knowing in their own way that Silver Star and Pumpkin Girl had saved the day yet again.

Tony Cooper lives in England and writes novels, comics and videogames while drinking tea. He has created a tie-in superhero comic featuring Hayley, and has most recently released a pair of graphic novels about psychopathic teenage murderers. He has also written and self-published two dark superhero novels, a comedy Sci-Fi novella and a short story collection. He still can't show any of his work to his mother. You, however, can see it by visiting **hungryblackbird.com**.

Against the Odds

A. A. Abbott

Jim was desperate for a smoke by the time the bus stopped. He felt around in the pockets of his suit, suddenly aware that it was straining at the seams. He'd put on weight since he last wore it.

The breeze was quickening, dark clouds rolling across a grey sky. He should get under cover soon to avoid the impending storm, and once he did, it was unlikely he'd be allowed a cigarette. Triumphantly, he fished out a crumpled packet with one stick left. The blast of nicotine calmed him as he strode down New Street. Stretching a quarter of a mile, the road was the spine of the city's shopping district. The stores didn't tempt him, but the chance of easy money did. Even more bookmakers had opened, garish red posters luring him with promises of wealth. He felt their pull, but managed to ignore them, focusing only on the ramp ahead. He couldn't afford to stop.

Everyone called it The Ramp, this concrete slope that led to the shops above the railway station. Jim hadn't understood why Eve wanted to meet him there, of all places. Two years before, the station and its unlovely shopping precinct had been swathed in white sheeting like a shroud. Now he saw it had really been a chrysalis, from which had emerged a giant glass bubble of boutiques and smart cafes.

He was actually impressed.

Half a decade and a lifetime of experience separated him from Eve. She was barely out of university, working for the charity as an intern. He'd only bothered listening to her on her first visit to the nick because he fancied her. She had a nice arse and amazing big eyes. Even though he quickly realised he had no chance – she was a born-again Christian and she had a fiancé – he still wanted to see her today. She was offering a mobile phone and a bus pass, all completely free. Anyway, now he was wearing a suit, she might find him attractive after all. He had to see his probation officer in an hour, so why not take a punt on a coffee with Eve first?

The new coffee shops looked posh. She'd chosen one where the drinks were a shocking price, over three pounds. That was okay for a beer, but out of order for a beverage that cost ten pence to make at home. It was criminal, really. Jim resolved to beat the beggars at their own game: he'd have tap water.

Eve persuaded him to order a filter coffee at ninety-nine pence. "Three sugars, please," he said.

She took some little brown packets from the counter.

"White sugar," he said, a touch snappish.

A smile played on her lips. "Sure," she agreed, swapping the sachets. She brought the tray of drinks to a table, unloading his filter coffee and a caramel latte with whipped cream for her. She was probably on expenses, he thought.

Silently, he watched as Eve sipped her drink, the cream forming a moustache above her soft red lips.

"Are you pleased to be out?" she asked.

He nodded. "Ecstatic."

Eve laughed. "Great. Well, here's your mobile phone." She handed him a box. "It's all charged, and I've programmed my number in it."

Jim could see right away that it was hardly top of the range. The charity's money was being wasted on too many lattes. "What about the bus pass?" he asked.

Eve frowned. "Head office says you don't need one. You're going to live with your mother in Newtown, aren't you? You can walk into the city centre from there."

"I'm not fit enough," he complained, outraged. He was sure she'd mentioned a bus pass before.

"You'll get fit." Eve's tone was jocular. She was trying to jolly him along. "Look, if your situation changes, ring me straight away, okay?"

A tinny rendition of *All Things Bright and Beautiful* floated out of her handbag. "Excuse me," she said.

Eve had an iPhone. The gulf between that and the cheap gadget she'd handed him was what made him lose it. As soon as she'd walked away from the table to take the call, turning her back on him, he took twenty pounds from the purse displayed invitingly in her open handbag.

She was just another mark, wasn't she? She shouldn't have left her bag with him like that; she was asking to be taken for a ride.

Pulling a face, Eve returned to her seat. "That was probation," she said. "Kevin is off sick. They can't find someone else to see you today. You're to visit them on Monday at ten instead."

"No worries," Jim said. If anything, he was relieved he didn't have to face the hassle yet. Kevin would insist on courses, jobcentre visits, benefits appointments. He could do without those, although he could use the benefits. The money in his pocket wouldn't last long, not unless he had a big win.

Eve looked at her watch. "Finished your coffee? I've got another meeting, I'm afraid. Will you be all right to get to your mum's?"

Jim resisted the urge to say a bus pass would help. Nodding, he stayed at the table, watching Eve's bum as she left the coffee shop, then staring at the shiny people shopping in the bright new complex. It looked futuristic, as if he had stepped out of the grey morning and into a time machine.

Eventually, he wandered back down the ramp and along New Street. His mouth twitched. The siren call of the bookies was harder to avoid now he was no longer under time pressure.

"Oi, Reverend! Want some?" A small man, his straw-coloured hair and beard straggly and dirty, was huddled at Jim's feet, a can of strong lager in his hand.

"Munchkin!" Jim grinned with joy. When he'd last walked past the mouth of this dingy concrete alley, Munchkin had been sitting on the edge of it, a Styrofoam cup in front of him to cadge change from passers-by. The knowledge that he was still here comforted Jim, helped him orientate himself in the present.

"Wanna do some preaching?" Munchkin asked. "You was always good at it."

Jim shrugged modestly. "The filth didn't think so."

"They won't be around this early," Munchkin said. "Here." He pulled a grimy cross from around his neck, with equally dirty hands. "Put that on."

"Okay," Jim said. "But if you're to take the collection for me, you need to smarten up." He looked doubtfully at Munchkin's bedraggled appearance.

"You got any cash?" Munchkin whined.

Jim sighed. "Suppose so."

They headed to the charity shops. Jim had to invest eight pounds on clothes for the little man, fifty pence on a bucket and another pound on scissors to cut the beard. He insisted Munchkin took a wash in the gents above the station.

"You'll do," he said shortly.

The spiel he gave shoppers on the corner of New Street and High Street was the same old gibberish. "The Lord is inviting you into his house. He has commanded me to build a church," he began.

Munchkin capered about, rattling the bucket, taking donations from anyone gullible enough to stop. It was a numbers game. Even at 11am on a Friday, there were plenty of shoppers; they only needed one in a hundred to make a contribution.

Munchkin whistled and nudged Jim in the ribs. "She likes you. I've took five pounds off her."

She was a girl of about twenty-five, blonder, prettier and more buxom than Eve. Jim's eyes were drawn to her long black dress and sleek stilettos. They looked expensive. What clinched it was the shopping bag from a designer boutique on New Street. It screamed money so much that he had to wave at her.

She waved back.

"Been buying something nice?" he mouthed.

The girl walked towards him. "Just my lunch in here," she said.

Close up, he could see he was right about the dress. It was very good quality, clearly designer. He liked that she had a sense of humour too.

"I'll buy you lunch," he offered, spotting a policeman marching past the Rotunda and deciding it was time to empty the bucket and leave. He scooped all the notes from it, leaving the hapless Munchkin with only loose change.

"You look very young to be a priest," she said. "I'm Marie, by the way."

"Jim." He was flattered. While he was only twenty-eight, prison had sprinkled grey hairs among his dark locks. He supposed that homelessness was worse; even scrubbed and tidy, Munchkin had aged, with more wrinkles and fewer teeth than Jim remembered.

Marie chose a cellar bar decorated in a florid Romanesque style, all columns and statues. To Jim's alarm, she asked for the dearest items on the menu.

He shrugged. It was a gamble, but wasn't everything in this life? Sometimes you had to spend money to make it.

A rather more pleasant surprise was meeting an old school friend. Ben wasn't just working behind the bar; he was managing it. "Come about the job?" he asked.

"Buying lunch," Jim said curtly.

Ben raised an eyebrow. "Well, the food's good. Free if you work in the kitchen. But I can see you don't need to, you've done well for yourself." He gave Jim two glasses of red wine with a wink. "On the house."

Jim knocked both drinks back before returning to Marie. The swift hit of booze softened the blow of having to pay for their meals in advance. He couldn't pull his usual stunt of avoiding the bill with a timely visit to the loo.

"I've brought you a glass of water," he told Marie.

"Thanks," she said, her blue eyes fixing on his. "Tell me about this church you're building."

"It'll be in Newtown," Jim said. "A rough area." He should know. "Of course, I must venture there for God's work, but it's not the sort of place a girl like you would go. I'm guessing you live somewhere like Solihull." He'd once had a lover in the well-heeled suburb to the south of the city, an older woman who'd eventually noticed the unexpected purchases on her credit card. It hadn't ended well.

"I live by Sutton Park."

He'd hit paydirt. Everyone was loaded in Sutton Coldfield. He began to daydream: about moving in with Marie, forging her signature and taking a loan against her flat. The cash, and lucky Jim, would be gone before she noticed.

"I'm thinking you're single?" he pressed.

Marie giggled. "I can't believe I'm being chatted up by a priest. This is so weird."

Food arrived. Marie happily tucked into a huge steak, following it with cheesecake. Jim concentrated on ogling her breasts. He managed to get her telephone number.

After they'd parted, he watched her walk past the alley where he'd met Munchkin. She took a package from her shopping bag, and handed it to a beggar lounging at the mouth of the alley. Jim couldn't see what it was; he guessed it was a sandwich she no longer needed.

Later, he looked in the window of the designer shop whose name was emblazoned on the bag. Marie was inside, serving a customer, a name badge on her prominent chest. Jim's mouth tightened. Who knew which end of Sutton Park she lived, and whether she even owned her flat? Marie was a shopgirl; he could guess the answers. He'd made a mark out of himself, gulled his own eyes into seeing only what he wanted to see.

He deserved a break. The bookie next door looked more inviting than ever. He'd feel better when the slot machines came good.

But they didn't.

He had no cash left even for a bus to Newtown; he had to walk, sighing and puffing.

Although he hadn't been away long, he didn't recognise the landscape. Derelict factories where he'd played as a child and smoked dope as a teenager were gone, shiny flats sprouting in their place. Jim imagined yuppies like Ben sitting on their balconies with a beer, watching as the city was remodelled around them.

Earlier, as the gates had shut behind him, he'd believed he was the same person returning to the same places he knew. Now Jim realised the world had changed, and so had he. For a start, he was out of condition, overweight after a stint in the prison kitchens with maximum carbohydrates and minimum exercise.

He was gasping for a cuppa, and even a hug from his mother, when he rang the doorbell of the dismal terrace where she lived. This, reassuringly, was stuck in a time warp, every bit as shabby as he remembered.

There was no warm welcome from her, however.

His stepfather, Barry, answered the door. "You're not coming in," he said, blocking the threshold.

"Where's Mum?"

"Out. And don't think she'd say different. She knows I'm not having you here, and that's that."

"Why not?" Jim was stunned. "It's all arranged with probation."

"Not anymore," Barry said. "You've pushed your luck once too often. The filth are looking for you." He sneered, his chin and pot belly wobbling. Topped by a bald head, his bulk loomed over Jim like an evil flesh-coloured blancmange. "That charity worker complained. Lady in the coffee shop saw you nick her money."

"I didn't," Jim said. It was an automatic response, although in truth he'd almost forgotten the theft.

"She won't press charges if you get a proper job. Like that'll happen, though. The Blues'll win the Champions' League first. I mean," he gestured at the tatty council house with its peeling paint and unkempt lawn, "we live in luxury here because I get off my arse and work."

"Such a palace," Jim muttered.

Barry eyeballed him. "Better than the nick, isn't it?" he spat. "Loser. When will you learn, the odds are stacked against you. The only winners are the bookies, the filth and the lawyers." He waved a fist. "Get out of my sight."

Jim trudged back to the city centre. He'd have to hook up with Munchkin once more, at least until the dole came through.

The narrow alley ran between two buildings and round the back of one of them. Munchkin, scruffy again within a matter of hours, was sniffing glue with a couple of dodgy friends.

"Oh, it's you," Munchkin mumbled, his eyes unfocused. "Whatcha want?"

"Share your pitch?" Jim asked hopefully.

Munchkin snarled at him. "Get lost," he said. "Unless you've brought me my money."

His friends jostled Jim. "Where's his money?"

"There isn't any," Jim said. He turned out his pockets.

"There's that phone," Munchkin said. "Must be worth something."

One of Munchkin's companions grabbed it with a sneer. "You owe it to the Munchster, right?" he said. "Now get out of here."

Darkness fell.

Jim found a doorway on New Street, and shivered there through the night, flinching from passers-by. For hours, he barely dozed. Eventually settling to sleep, he was woken by a distant Nokia ring-tone.

The morning chill assailed him, and his stomach rumbled. Jim flicked his eyelids open. In front of him stood ten toes, nails immaculately painted, peeping from black patent stilettoes. Jim's gaze travelled up the slim, tanned limbs above them, the expensive red dress, and finally, Marie's face, frowning as she jabbed at her smartphone.

Her puzzled expression softened. Leaning down, she pressed a two-pound coin into his hand. "Get a coffee," she said.

Pity was all she had left for him.

Freedom hadn't brought easy money, or love.

He looked away, biting his lip.

Feeling lightheaded, Jim walked past the betting shops, to the ramp. He bought a ninety-nine pence filter coffee, loaded it with four sugars, then sat, nursing it, for two hours before returning to the cellar bar. After all, he had kitchen experience. Ben had told him there was a job going. What were the odds of getting it?

It must be worth a punt.

Thriller writer AA Abbott was born in Luton, but did her growing up in Birmingham. Set in Brum and London, her crime thrillers sizzle with suspense, twists and the evils of office politics. Check out her Trail series for stories of revenge, murder and vodka. Find out more at **aaabbott.co.uk** *and connect on* Twitter *and* Facebook *as* **@AAAbbottStories**.

New Street Blues

Andrew Sparke

The old guard are marching up New Street,
young men in scarlet attire,
wishing themselves swiving indoors instead
of parading like yesteryear's men.
Moving in unison, rigid,
not even a quarter beat off,
cheered on by no more than a motley array
of the self-unemployed and the bored.
The freedom afforded to soldiers
to march unfettered up roads
more usually cluttered with traffic,
with buses, taxis and cars,
is seldom given to others,
who must jostle a way through the crowds
to reach destinations desired:
a favourite teashop or store.
Without deals illicit and lawful,
New Street might just fade away.
No-one would come here for reasons
of leisure, enjoyment and play,
when for smiling, drunken delusions
they could wander up Broad Street instead,
or follow canal-side to Gas Street,
finding some warmth in a pub.
For New Street is old, wet and windy,
unlike the station bearing its name,
which masks the old concrete tunnels
in new tiles and steel and paint.
But the trains haven't changed in the revamp,

nor have Brummies ever outgrown
the war with their Yam-Yam cousins,
played out in football and jeers.
Who was it invented the Balti?
Who was it first smelted pig iron?
Who was it first played metal music?
And where has the money all gone?
It hasn't brought riches to New Street,
and the Black Country is hiding its wealth.
The buildings are unchanged in decades,
bearing their smog-raddled scars.
But if it didn't happen in New Street,
in Moseley, Sparkbrook or Shard End,
then as far as it matters round here,
it has no importance at all.
The insularity natural
to those who have little to lose,
out-faced by the capital's yahoos
and drowning their sorrows in booze.
It's a no-man's-land in the struggle
eternal between North and South.
We call it the heart of old England,
but in truth, it lies from its mouth.

Andrew Sparke is a reformed solicitor now turned writer-publisher. He writes about relationships affected by crime in two novels, Abuse Cocaine & Soft Furnishings *and* Copper Trance & Motorways *with a third underway. He also dabbles in something akin to poetry. His imprint APS Books now publishes nearly 50 other authors. See* **andrewsparke.com** *for publishing and* **bellawychelm.com***, his specialist website for the real life unsolved 1940s body-in-a-tree mystery.*

New Street Station

Dawn Abigail

The silver serpent snakes around,
surrounded by a symphony of sound,
of trains and feet and *beep-beep-beep*.
Faster, faster; too slow, too slow,
people come and people go.
The centre of the centre is
new New Street

Lights and colour
and a gleam like no other
from sky and ground and all around
the shops set out their goods to see.
All to call *buy me, buy me!*
Grand Central at
new New Street

A sheltering space,
a meeting place
of rumble, rustle, hustle and bustle.
All cultures, all races
from all sorts of places,
the heart of England beats
at new New Street.

Dawn Abigail has been writing poetry for as long as she can remember. With a creative background as an actor, improviser and storyteller, Dawn has been known to shout her words at crowds in various major cities around the UK. Dawn has joined forces with London based Calligrapher, Gwyneth Hibbett, to produce art cards and prints of their original work. Their book of beautifully illuminated, lighthearted poetry, called Deeply Meaningful Poetry for Very Serious People, *is due out in early 2019.*

Pest Control

T. K. Elliott

Chapter One

"We get all the exotic places," Gilbertson said, looking around at the dismal corridor with the wire gates in front of them. "Forget Iraq, Afghanistan. We get an old mail tunnel under Birmingham New Street Station."

"You're better off here," Faraday rumbled. "Sand gets in everything." In black overalls, Faraday blended into the shadows until he smiled – it reminded Dinah of the Cheshire Cat, a white smile hanging in the air.

Dinah could relate to Gilbertson's complaint. They were the UK's only Special Forces 'weird shit' team – official designation: Atypical Situation Management Team – and they'd gone up against a demon-summoning coven and won. They'd fought vampires and won. They'd faced off against the fae and won. Now... vermin in a tunnel. Part of her hoped it would turn out to be something more exciting.

"Okay," she said, glancing at each member of the team in turn. "Faraday, you're with me. You stay here, Q. Gilbertson can come with me – he runs faster."

McQuaid nodded; he ran faster than most fifty-year-olds, but that might not be fast enough. They'd been called because a pest control operative had been sent into the tunnel after reports of vermin and hadn't come back out – and neither had the station employee sent in to find out what had happened to him.

Gilbertson's green eyes lit up, but he said nothing more than, "Okay, Doc." He knelt and opened his aluminium briefcase, unpacking the communications headsets and handing them out; McQuaid knelt beside him, putting on his headset and then adjusting the controls in preparation for his role as 'home base'.

Dinah took off her hard hat and put on the headset, positioning the HUD earpiece, then settling the hat over it, making sure that her hair was pinned up out of the way. She tucked a black strand out of her eyes.

"Okay everyone, comms check." Q's voice came through, oddly doubled since she could hear it normally as well as through the earpiece. The HUD lit up, displaying a cartoon wizard drawn in green lines; Gilbertson had done the original setup, and his sense of humour was sometimes questionable.

"Doc, loud and clear," she said. "HUD A-OK. Over."

The others confirmed that their headsets were also in working order. She took a breath. "All right. Faraday, you take point with the flamethrower. Then you, Gilbertson; you're in charge of keeping Q in the loop. You take the Taser. I'll bring up the rear."

She glanced down at Dog, who blinked up at her and opened his mouth to reveal dozens of long, sharp teeth. He resembled nothing so much as a black wolf big enough to eat a Shetland pony and still have room for dessert; between claws, teeth, and sheer mass, Dog was one of the better-armed members of the team. "Dog, you go up front with Faraday."

Faraday nodded at Dog, who stared back and blinked slowly. Dog liked Faraday – but he also liked yanking the big man's chain.

"All right. We're looking for signs of whatever this is, or where it might be from. Anything unusual, we stop. We evaluate. And if we don't like it, we run like fuck." Dinah made eye contact with each team member. "Clear?"

Nod.

Nod.

Nod.

Dog's eyes glowed red.

McQuaid unlocked the gates, and he and Faraday pushed them open with a squeal of hinges. They sorted themselves into order, Faraday going first with the nozzle of his flamethrower ready, Dog at his side.

The tunnel had riveted metal ribs framing a rounded cross-section, and a flat floor. Although the emergency lights halfway up the walls were on, they each switched on their helmet lamps. Their steps echoed, and the helmet lamps made the shadows dip and slide.

In front of her, Gilbertson kept up a continuous murmur to McQuaid. Dinah drew her wand, her sweaty palm making the smooth wood slick. She was beyond the stage of feeling ridiculous holding a stick like a weapon. *Flame-thrower. Taser. Stick. Yeah, right.*

She had no idea what had got the pest control guy, but it had to be something that could either kill a man so fast that he didn't have time to run, or disable him, then kill him slowly.

Faraday's boots hit the ground regularly; the most combat-experienced in the team, he had started his army career in the Parachute Regiment, then transferred to 22 SAS. McQuaid had spent more than twenty years as an engineer in REME; Gilbertson was Signals. The Boss was Adjutant General's Corps – he wielded a mean spreadsheet and knew how to do double-entry accounting; he'd stayed behind for this one. She was the newest member of the team, badged Intelligence Corps, and her Comparative Mythology PhD was turning out to be a far more practical study than she had expected.

"We got corpse," Faraday said laconically. "You want to check it out, Doc?"

"Okay. Cover me." Still gripping her wand, she moved past Gilbertson.

"*Lux,*" she murmured, and the tip of her wand glowed enough to allow a better examination.

She swallowed, bile rising in her throat as she crouched.

Since she'd got involved in this, she'd seen a lot of corpses in various states of integrity. This one could have been worse.

The man had been reduced to a skeleton, the remains of his station uniform shredded as if *something* had torn through to get to the flesh. The bones were picked clean of flesh and tendon, and cross-hatched with scratch marks, as if from teeth. Dinah swallowed, feeling sick. Could there be anything worse than being eaten alive?

She reached out and touched the rags of skeleton's jacket then rubbed it between her fingers.

Slimy. The bones – in places – were slimy too.

"It was fast, I think," she said, thankful that her voice didn't shake or squeak. She indicated the position of the corpse. "He was running back to the station; it caught him, brought him down, and – and ate him. It seems likely it's got a lot of small teeth, or claws – lots of tiny marks on the bones, no large ones. And the clothes are slimy." She sat back on her heels. "Did it leave a trail?"

Faraday crouched down and touched the floor with one hand. Then he stood, wiping his palm on his overall. "Affirmative," he said.

Dinah picked up a wave of *yuck* from him that didn't show on his impassive face. The useful parts of being a psychomancer, she reflected, were often outweighed by the disadvantages. Telepathy, empathy and mind control sounded great until you realised that they came with a side-order of potential insanity – and the ability to feel other people's disgust.

She frowned. "We'll have to look for tracks. See if it just left the slime, or if there are signs of feet. And we need to find the pest control guy. On we go. Faraday, stay sharp."

"Right you are, Doc."

Faraday's calm tone reminded her that he knew this shit. Plus, she ought to try to keep it together. She stood up and wiped her hands, transferring the wand from one to the other, glad she was the only one who could feel other people's emotions. "Let's go."

This time, she bent down as they went, casting her glow near the floor. The slime trail was as wide as the tunnel.

Only a few more yards, and her light picked up another skeleton, this one in an overall.

"We've found the pest control guy," she said, and felt stupid. Obvious, much?

Dog's ears pricked, and she felt the rumble of his subvocal growl through the soles of her boots. She stopped, and Faraday glanced back at her.

"There's something up ahead," she breathed. She closed her eyes and forced herself to be calm. She let her mind flow outwards, past Faraday and Gilbertson, instantly recognisable; she thought of minds as blobs of coloured light – Gilbertson was gold and green, and Faraday was red and brown. Dog, on the other hand, was a violent roil of black, more intense than either of the men.

Walls and distance meant nothing in what Dinah had learned to call the 'psychosphere'; she could travel miles in moments, and buildings could be anything from completely invisible to a monolith of multi-coloured fire. It was fascinating, and it was dangerous because if *you* could see *it, it* could see *you.*

This time, she didn't have to go far: just beyond the curve of the tunnel was another mind – a trembling pink cloud with little gold sparkles. It didn't react to Dinah's mental presence, so either the mind's owner was good at hiding his or her feelings – probably her, Dinah thought – or she couldn't detect Dinah's presence. Dinah retreated and opened her eyes.

"One person around the corner," she said. "Probably female." She glanced from Faraday and Dog to Gilbertson. "Gilbertson, you hang back behind. Faraday, you ready?"

Faraday nodded. Dog grinned, showing teeth.

"Okay, then." At Dinah's nod, they moved forward.

Dinah was slightly ahead when they rounded the curve, wand at the ready. She and Faraday came to a halt so suddenly that Gilbertson bumped into her.

The mind she had seen belonged to an Asian girl who looked about eighteen, wearing a station uniform with a customer service jacket and a black hijab. She stared at them, her eyes going from Faraday, armed and dangerous, to Dog, whose lips were pulled back from his teeth and whose subterranean growl was now audible.

Then the girl moved her hands in a fast circle, and white fire burned afterimages onto Dinah's retinas. She was still blinking when she heard the girl's scream; Faraday's "Fuck!" and Gilbertson's "Holy shit!" came a second later.

Dinah's vision cleared, and for a moment, her brain refused to process what her eyes saw.

At first, she thought it was water – a wave of white surf, tumbling out of a portal in the air where the girl had been standing.

Then she realised it wasn't.

It was worms. Thousands of worms, ranging in size from only a few inches in length to several feet.

"Gilbertson! Run!" she yelled. She brought her wand down, screaming, "*Ignis!*"

Fire spewed from her wand as Faraday activated the flame-thrower. Two lances of flame shot out, but despite the stink of burned flesh, there were too many of the worms – they came on and on, crawling over the crisped black corpses of their relatives, too fast, and too many of them, for the fire to reach them all.

"Faraday! Go!" she gasped.

The flame-thrower coughed and died, and his footsteps retreated too, as she hosed the oncoming tide of worms with fire one last time.

She ran.

She sprinted along the tunnel, Dog loping beside her. She saw the end of the tunnel, then McQuaid and

Gilbertson standing to one side, silhouetted against the light; Faraday had nearly reached them.

The gloop and susurration of the worms behind her was getting closer. She dug deeper, pouring every ounce of effort into running.

Then they were under her feet; she skidded, their soft bodies moving under her soles. She felt their tiny teeth tugging at her overalls, but unlike the luckless pest control man, hers were Nomex/Kevlar, designed for high-impact tactical operations. Even so, if she fell, she'd be dead, because they'd go for her exposed face and hands.

She staggered and hit the wall, and brought her wand around in a swipe, screaming "*Vi!*" She swept the worms clear with raw force, then pushed off, stumbling into a run again.

She burst through into the light, and the gates clanged shut behind her and McQuaid locked them.

She slumped to the floor, leaning her back against the wall and her arms across her raised knees. After a moment, she straightened up and watched the worms retreat, leaving a trail of slime.

"Well, *fuck.*"

Dog came over to her, wagging his tail. In front of her, he dropped a single worm. As soon as it hit the floor, the thing made for her with blind, single-minded determination.

"Shit!" She scooted away on her backside. "Gilbertson! Your briefcase!"

Gilbertson dumped the electronics out and slid the aluminium case across to her, and she leaned over and flipped the foot-long worm into it with the end of her wand, then slammed it shut.

"What the *hell* are those?" McQuaid's Scottish accent was stronger than usual.

"Fucked if I know." Dinah rested the back of her head against the wall. "But we get to find out. Hoo-rah."

Chapter Two

"Dholes." Dinah pinched the bridge of her nose and squeezed her eyes shut. Her stomach had the gnawing feeling of too much coffee.

"You what?"

"We've got dholes. Carnivorous worms covered in slime." Dinah pushed the leather-bound copy of *Bestiary of the Uncannie* across the library table to Gilbertson. The library in the house Dinah had inherited was huge; it even had a catalogue: unfortunately, the catalogue – like many of the volumes – was handwritten.

Gilbertson squinted at the text. "It says here, they grow to *hundreds of feet in length.*"

At that moment, a crash and a yell sounded from the cellar, and Dinah ran for the door, followed by Gilbertson. She took the steps down to the cellar two at a time and saw Faraday stamping on something on the floor, and McQuaid aiming a carbon dioxide fire extinguisher at the big table, producing a hissing cloud of white vapour.

"What is it?" she demanded.

"Jesus H. Fucking Christ!" Faraday yelped.

McQuaid turned, trailing carbon dioxide, and Dinah saw what Faraday had on the floor. There were three bits of worm wriggling determinedly away from each other, and one squished mess of ichor.

Dinah drew her wand and snapped, "*Ignis,*" sending a lance of flame at one of the worm-bits as Faraday leaped backwards. She scored a direct hit, gagging as the smell of charred meat wafted up. She held her breath as she looked for the other two pieces. She spotted one but wasn't as fast as Dog, who brought a paw down on it, then ate it. He gave her a smug look. Turning back, she was just in time to see the third worm bit wriggle under a cupboard. She pointed. "Move that, Faraday, Gilbertson!"

The two men hurried over to the cupboard and dragged it away from the wall, exposing the piece of worm, which tried to hide under the cupboard again. Dinah caught it with another blast of flame and then turned back to McQuaid, who had transferred the worm remains from the floor to a metal tray on the table, where he had a larger piece that looked blanched. Cautiously, she poked it with her wand; it didn't move.

"I think it's dead, ma'am," McQuaid said. "I froze it with the fire extinguisher."

"Good thinking," she said. She turned back to Faraday. "And what were *you* doing, Kev?"

Faraday shrugged. "Sorry, Doc. When we cut the worm up to dissect it, we found that the pieces can act independently. They'll also eat each other if there's nothing else available, and they're quite resistant to being stamped on."

Gilbertson came over to stare at the dead worm bits on the tray. "Shit. How do you get rid of something like that?"

"Damned if I know," Dinah sighed. "If these are dead, I suggest we go back upstairs and see what we can come up with."

She led the way back up to the library and handed *Bestiary of the Uncannie* to McQuaid as they took their seats around the big fireplace. The library was exactly like a library ought to be: lots of shelves of leather-bound books, ladders to get to the upper shelves, and comfortable leather-upholstered chairs clustered around a fireplace. Currently, the library even had a large dog stretched out in front of the fire: Dinah was surprised that Dog's fur didn't catch light.

"Dholes," she said. She took a tin of brownies out of the fireside cupboard, opened it, and put it on the floor between the chairs. "As we've found, fire kills them. According to the book, they don't like bright light. So we probably don't have to worry about them taking to the streets."

McQuaid tapped the open book. "They can tunnel. Most of the soil in Birmingham's too sandy for good tunnels, but worms that live underground may not be concerned about tunnels collapsing. Or they could use the sewers."

"Joy." Dinah leaned back in her chair. "They're fast, they're carnivorous, and they can tunnel under your house and come up to eat you during the night."

"So where do they come from?" Gilbertson asked. "I mean, giant man-eating worms. If they were a common problem, it'd be pretty hard to hide." He took a brownie and inspected it suspiciously. "Hey, I didn't know you baked, Doc."

"It's not toxic," she protested. "I can cook." Up until she'd inherited the house, she hadn't cooked much, but the big kitchen begged to be used.

"I'm sure they're fine," McQuaid said. "But my wife won't like it if I put on weight."

"I'll have one in a bit," Faraday put in with a grin. "How're you doing, Gilbertson?"

Gilbertson shook his head and swallowed. "Don't risk it, Sarge; the team needs you. I'll heroically sacrifice myself in your stead." He took another brownie.

"That's okay, guys," Dinah said. "If you're worried, you needn't eat them. I'll just take them away..." She stood up.

"Oh, no, no need for that," Faraday said immediately. "I was just... just... increasing the anticipation. I think it's at the right level now." He reached out and took a brownie out of the tin.

"So, where *do* they come from, Doc?" Gilbertson repeated.

"Elsewhere," Dinah said, waving a hand.

"Oh. Fuck."

Dinah was still trying to get her head around *Elsewhere*. She thought of it as lots of bubbles, connected by bridges; there was *here* which was one bubble, and there was *elsewhere* which was every other bubble. She'd been to some. The fae lived in a series of interlinked, closely-related bubbles. Dog had come from another one.

71

Evidently the worms – the dholes – came from yet another. Or maybe Dog came from the same one; he hadn't seemed bothered by them.

"If we can find the bridge, I should be able to close it," she said. "Then we're left with the ones here. Fire seems to work. Napalm might be better. Q, can you rig us something that will spray napalm?"

McQuaid nodded. "I can do that."

"How fast?" Dinah asked.

"By tomorrow, if Kev gives me a hand."

Dinah glanced across at Faraday, who nodded. "Sure. If they came across a bridge, who built it? They don't look like they could do it themselves."

"If two dimensions get close enough, or are similar enough, a bridge can just *happen*."

"So New Street Station is similar to a hell dimension full of flesh-eating worms?"

Dinah grinned. "I'm a Birmingham girl. Once you've been replatformed twice for the same train..." She sobered. "It doesn't seem likely, though. Gilbertson – how are you coming with identifying the girl in the tunnel?"

Gilbertson finished his second brownie and took another. "Fazia Ahmed. Eighteen years old. Worked at New Street since leaving college. Customer services." He shoved the rest of the brownie into his mouth and passed his laptop to her.

On the screen was a Facebook profile with a picture of the girl they'd seen in the tunnel. "That's her," Dinah agreed. "What else do we know about her?" She passed the laptop back.

Dinah saw the laptop screen change and guessed that Gilbertson had managed to hack into the station's computer system.

Gilbertson scrolled through some text. He grimaced. "It's pretty awful. She got racial abuse off a bunch of passengers. They got her surrounded, and ripped her hijab off – a couple of her colleagues rescued her, and charges were pressed, but she had time off work for stress. Then she went back, and it happened again – not as bad, but she cracked up and had to go home."

"But what about magic? Do we have any connection?"

Gilbertson shrugged. "Not really, Doc, but she's Muslim and pretty devout. I looked it up, and Islam is pretty much against magic. I don't reckon she'd be hanging out down the pub with the rest of the magical community."

"You're probably right." Dinah frowned. "And when she opened that bridge in the tunnel, it was sloppy."

"What do you mean?" Faraday asked curiously.

"Some spells, if you're sloppy, you get bleed-over," Dinah said. "Sometimes heat, but often visible light. That flash when she opened the bridge – it shouldn't have happened."

"Well, that's good, isn't it?" Gilbertson said. "She'll be easier to beat."

"Not necessarily," Faraday said, shaking his head. "You know who the best swordsman fears?"

"Go on," Gilbertson said.

"He doesn't fear the second-best swordsman. He fears the *worst* swordsman because he doesn't know what the fucker's going to do."

"Oh," Gilbertson said.

"And we don't even know if *Fazia* knows what she's going to do." Dinah shuddered, remembering a few incidents from her own childhood. She didn't know whether to consider herself lucky or not that her primary talent was psychomancy: although she hadn't set fire to herself or opened a portal that allowed carnivorous worms to escape into her bedroom, her mind had nearly broken under the strain. She'd been told that most young mages born into non-mage families died young – was Fazia at the dangerous stage where she had the power, but no control, and no idea what was happening to her?

"So what do we do?" McQuaid asked. "She's a kid; I've got a daughter that age! We can't just treat her as a threat if she doesn't even know what she's doing."

"Yes, we can," Faraday said. "She *is* a threat."

"We have to," Dinah said. She glanced at McQuaid. "*But* we can try to talk her down first. I don't want to kill her either, but we may have to."

She remembered all too vividly the terror and despair of not knowing what was going on in her own head, of being afraid that she was going mad. She had been lucky; her foster parents had sent their troublesome charge off to karate lessons with an instructor who had insisted that his students learn to meditate. This had had the side-effect of giving her the tools to keep her own thoughts in her head and other people's out of it. She looked across at Gilbertson. "What else do we know about her? Work record? Disciplinary?"

"Not much. She's quiet, doesn't get involved with her colleagues much – except her father, who works there too. He's a cleaner. Only one thing: people have complained they couldn't find her, particularly on Fridays. It was suspected she was going off to pray, but nobody ever saw her either coming or going."

"But if she can build bridges..."

"She could appear and disappear whenever she wanted," Gilbertson finished. "What I can't understand is why she did it. I mean, carnivorous worms from another dimension are kind of cool, in a Lovecraft sort of way, but why?"

McQuaid nodded. "Boy's got a point. Assuming she did it on purpose."

Dinah gave in to Dog's soft brown eyes and gave him a brownie. He ate it in one bite and resumed the *I-am-starving* routine. She gave him another. "I think we have to assume the worst. You do that kind of thing either because it's cool to watch, or because of the results. That tunnel wasn't near anywhere – and the gates kept the dholes in."

"So, it wasn't going to accomplish anything." Faraday brushed crumbs off his fingers – pointlessly, because he immediately took another brownie. "No casualties. Nowhere for the dholes to go. They'd starve – or start eating each other, then die."

"And in that case," Dinah said, "this is part of something else. It must have been a – a practice run."

"I bet the plan's to open one of those bridges right in the middle of the concourse at rush hour," Gilbertson said. "That's what I'd do if I'd gone through what she did. *Die, fuckers.*"

Chapter Three

"Okay, let's do it," Dinah said, rubbing her hands against her thighs; she stopped when she realised she was doing it.

The two thousand-lumen lamps bolted to her Kevlar helmet were heavy enough to make it feel precariously balanced. She reached up and switched them on; the corridor lit up as the rest of the team followed suit, the glare bleaching out the dim safety lights.

The dholes had gone – at least from the part of the tunnel Dinah could see. Had they retreated into their own dimension? Had Fazia closed the bridge already? Hopefully, the team could just check the tunnel and leave, *then* work out what to do about Fazia.

The Station Manager had at first refused to believe that Fazia – a nice, quiet girl – would ever attack anyone. She'd also refused to close the station, pointing out that Dinah had no proof that Fazia *would* attempt to stage any kind of violent incident – even though, the Station Manager admitted, Fazia had not turned up for work and hadn't called in sick either. Dinah had argued that *proof* would be when Fazia actually did it, when it would be too late, but this hadn't done any good.

Dinah swallowed, trying to ignore the sick pre-combat feeling in her stomach. This wasn't the simple monster-in-the-tunnel problem they'd thought it was; it was a potential disaster, and it was her job to limit it. Somehow.

The first task, she reminded herself, was getting rid of the dholes and the bridge.

None of the dholes could be allowed to survive. They bred quickly, as long as food was available. Dinah had the sudden crazy idea of blocking up the tunnel and leaving it until only one huge, fat dhole was left.

No. That's the sort of plan that's bound to go wrong. Kill them all now.

McQuaid unlocked the gate. Faraday, Dinah, and Dog went first, followed by Gilbertson and McQuaid. Dinah had decided that although safety usually dictated leaving a man behind to manage any rescue operations, this time, it would better to have all five of them on hand to deal with the dholes.

All three men had flamethrowers modified for napalm; Dog had teeth and didn't seem to be in any doubt as to their efficacy against dholes.

Their boots hit the floor in time, a determined military march; Dinah could feel the others' tension, like a buzzing at the back of her mind. She looked from side to side, searching for signs of magic. She *should* be able to spot the bridge.

Dog began to growl, and then they heard it – the whispering rush as the dholes approached.

"Ready," Dinah said. She drew her wand.

And the dholes came around the curve, a knee-high wave of wriggling, slithering white worms.

And the tide slowed.

The wriggling became more frantic, and the worms seemed to try to collapse in on themselves.

"Move it forward!" she snapped.

Some of the dholes appeared to be trying to retreat, or burrow beneath the top layer. But the advance had stopped. Unfortunately, what they'd hoped – that the dholes would retreat – wasn't happening. Maybe it was like a crowd at a football stadium, the dholes at the back wouldn't let the front dholes retreat.

"Okay – *fire*," Dinah snapped.

Three jets of napalm and her lance of blue-white flame shot out, momentarily hiding the dholes from view.

The fire did not set the dholes alight, but the burning napalm did kill the ones it reached and charred the bodies. The other problem, she realised, was that the tunnel was an enclosed space, which gave them a limited time to use fire. It was probably large enough that lack of oxygen would not be a survival problem, but the heat would become unbearable.

"Okay, cut the napalm. Move in," she ordered.

They moved in, towards the charred dholes, the blackened surface ones still shifting as the live ones underneath churned. Dinah stared around, searching for the bridge – it *had* to be there!

And it was. A circular shape in the air; through the opening she saw piles of bones. The bones from what?

"Found it," she said, pointing. "Against the wall. Cover me."

The dholes had stopped coming through, the light and fire driving them back from the gateway between the tunnel and their own dimension. Dinah moved forwards, reaching the edge of the tide of dholes, and started kicking them aside, trusting her overall's fireproofing to protect her from the still-burning napalm. She felt their tiny, sharp teeth scraping against her boots and overalls, and shuddered.

She took a deep breath. She wasn't good at this – she didn't enjoy practising creating bridges because she never quite knew what she was going to find on the other side. Closing them was easier, though.

Dinah raised her wand, and carefully concentrated her thoughts and her will.

"*Occludo*," she whispered.

As she moved her wand in a careful circle, the bridge began to close as if she was zipping up a bag; it vanished in a shower of sparks and a wave of released energy, producing a concussion on the air.

"That it, Doc?" Faraday asked.

"It's closed," she confirmed. "Now we get rid of them."

They worked in grim silence. It was hot, dirty work; the live dholes fought to get away from the light and the fire, but they also burrowed under the dead ones and ate the corpses. The stench of burned flesh and guts and ichor made Dinah gag, and she knew the rest of the team didn't feel any better. In fact, their nausea made hers worse.

This has got to be one of the most disgusting jobs we've ever had, she thought as McQuaid and Faraday shovelled dead dholes aside. Gilbertson was scraping the corpses further back, to keep the dead separated from the living. The napalm had worked well, but had run out – now Dinah's spells were the only source of fire. Her stomach rumbled: she'd need chocolate soon – once she got the taste of charred dhole out of her mouth.

"Doc!"

Gilbertson's urgent voice dragged her attention away from the dholes; it was a relief to be able to halt the fire spell, if only for a moment. She looked back, and he tapped his earpiece. "Station Manager," he said. "I'll transfer."

Dinah's earpiece crackled to life as she stuck her wand back in her belt. "Dinah Penhallow," she said crisply. "What I can do for you, ma'am?"

"Fazia's on the concourse!" the woman's voice came through, speaking fast, crackling slightly. "I've told the police she's a suspected terrorist."

Fuck, what? "Ma'am?"

"The police will deal with it. We've got an armed unit here."

Dinah clenched her teeth to avoid her scream of frustration escaping to where it could make the situation more fucked up than it already was. "I see," she said, because there wasn't much else to be said. "We'll be up there in two minutes." She closed her eyes for a moment. Was there any way she could rescue this? "If her father's on shift, get him down there. And an imam, if you can."

She ended the call and turned back to the others. "Station Manager's told the police Fazia's a terrorist," she said flatly. "We need to get up there ASAP. The rest of the dholes are going to have to wait."

Chapter Four

Dinah stared down over the glass barrier. Fazia was standing by one of the white pillars on the main concourse, dressed in jeans, long-sleeved *Birmingham City FC* hoodie, and hijab. "I hope she bottles it," Dinah said.

Faraday shook his head. "She won't. She's just working up the courage."

It had taken just over two minutes to get up to the concourse; they had stripped off their fireproof gear, leaving it with McQuaid, who was guarding the tunnel. Gilbertson had gone to fetch Faraday's rifle, although Dinah hoped he wouldn't have to use it.

She'd contacted the senior officer of the station's police team, but he hadn't been willing to work with her team without authorisation. The request was probably still working its way up the layers of bureaucracy.

If the police moved in, the situation would get complicated. They'd treat Fazia as a vanilla terrorist, and if she *was* just a scared young mage, Dinah couldn't think of a better way to push the girl over the edge. Then the range of options would narrow drastically: there weren't many ways to stop an out-of-control mage short of lethal force. The only question would be how many other people would die. Hence Faraday's rifle: a rifle in the hands of a sharpshooter was the safest – for everyone but the mage.

Dinah made her way down the escalator to the main concourse, her stomach tying itself in knots. She kept an eye on Fazia, not wanting the girl to disappear into the Friday rush hour crowd. In her peripheral vision, she saw station staff ushering members of the public off the concourse: good. There was one police officer keeping an eye on Fazia; the others were out of sight – probably developing an action plan or talking to their control centre.

Above her, Faraday would be clearing bystanders from his location.

She stepped off the escalator and approached the girl, hands in her jacket pockets. She wanted to look casual – hands visible might be reassuring to someone used to dealing with weapons, but it wasn't to someone used to magic. She wished she had thought to transfer her Glock to her pocket from the holster in the small of her back beneath her jacket, but it was too late now. She lowered her mental shields slightly, allowing the emotions washing through the concourse to reach her.

She managed not to sway as the storm hit her.

Big crowds had always been a problem – less so now she could control her magic better – but this was special. There was fear, from the station staff and the customers who were being ushered away. A bright point of cold resolve that was Faraday. And a whirling maelstrom of fear, pain, and anger from Fazia.

She knew the instant Fazia noticed her. The girl stiffened and took a small step back against the pillar, her fear spiking into terror. Dinah stopped about ten metres away. She licked her lips; this was where it would start to go right, or wrong.

"Hi," she said.

"Who are you?" Fazia's voice was high and breathy. "You're not a pest control person, are you?"

Dinah grinned. "Well, yes and no. Me and my team deal with more exotic problems. But flesh-eating worms were a first." The concourse was gradually emptying, but not fast enough. Fazia's fear was bad; it increased the chance she would kick off. "Where did you find them?"

"I didn't do anything!"

Dinah shrugged. "Well, somebody did. They're called dholes. The only way they'd get here is if somebody built a bridge – it isn't bad enough here to form a natural resonance."

"You don't know *anything*! You don't know what it's like!"

"So, tell me."

If the girl was talking, she wasn't opening bridges. How much control did Fazia have? How many places could she reach? Had she discovered how to bridge between two locations in the same dimension? "I know it's been tough. Nobody should have to put up with that kind of crap. It's not such a problem for me; I'm half Japanese, so people often just assume I'm a tourist."

"And you're not Muslim," Fazia said. She touched her hijab as if reassuring herself it was still there. "Why do people care if I wear hijab? Even the Queen wears a headscarf!"

"I don't get it either," Dinah admitted. Out of the corner of her eye, she saw a figure in police tactical gear. If she couldn't de-escalate this quickly, it was going to go south.

She concentrated on calmness, trying to push the feeling out towards Fazia. If she tried anything more overt, Fazia might notice and spook, so she continued speaking. "I think it's fear. People are afraid of things they don't understand. It's why people kill spiders."

Dinah took a step forwards and relaxed slightly when Fazia didn't move. "It's not very consoling to be told that if you react, you play into their hands – but unfortunately, it's true. Somebody has to be the adult, and if it's not them, that leaves you."

Then she saw it: one of the police team was creeping up behind Fazia. No! Not *now*! Not when Fazia was starting to relax – starting to listen.

The man reached out and grabbed her – and Fazia screamed and tore away, one hand reaching out. Fire exploded from her, enveloping him, and Fazia disappeared.

The police officer staggered backwards, his screams echoing in the now-silent concourse. He fell, rolling, his cries fading to moans and his movements becoming weaker.

Dinah retched as the smell of burned meat reached her; the concourse was silent for a moment as the impact of what had just happened sank in.

Then the screaming started.

Dinah looked around frantically; was Fazia still in the station – or not? *Fuck, fuck, fuck.*

The station staff had not yet cleared the concourse, and the relatively orderly evacuation was in disarray. People were yelling, running; near one of the doors, a fight had broken out, blocking the exit.

More screaming.

Dinah looked around frantically, and spotted Fazia on the mezzanine level. It had been cleared of public; that was one small mercy. Unfortunately, the girl was now diagonally across the concourse from Faraday and on the wrong side of a pillar. He didn't have a clear shot.

"Fazia!" Dinah shouted up to the girl. "Think what you're doing! There isn't any need for this – we can talk, find some way through."

"You're lying!" The girl screamed back. She sounded as though she were crying. "You don't want to help me – you just want to stop me! Well, you're not going to stop me! I can't stand it – I can't take it anymore! I'm sick of being told to *go home* – I was *born here*. Birmingham is my home! Why can't I walk down the street wearing what I want, like everybody else? Why is it okay to walk down the street with your muffin top rolls of fat showing, or your breasts practically bursting out of your top, but it's not okay to wear a headscarf?" Fazia laughed bitterly. "Oh, I forgot – it's only not okay to wear a headscarf if you're Muslim. *You* said those – those *things* could only come here if where they came from was like here! Well, it *is!* I didn't want them – but they just *came!*"

Fazia whirled as a member of staff from one of the food concessions started to inch towards her. "Keep away!" she screamed. Flame burst from her hand again, setting fire to tables and cracking the safety glass intended to stop people falling over the edge.

Dinah glanced back as she heard footsteps behind her. The pale-faced Station Manager was approaching with an older Asian man in a station uniform.

"This is Wahid Ahmed – Fazia's father."

Dinah nodded. "Thanks – you'd better keep out of the way now. Mr Ahmed, what can you tell me?"

"This is not like her, it's not," he said, sounding lost. "She's a sweet girl, a lovely girl. How could she do this?"

"Oh, Daddy," Fazia wailed.

He stared up at her. "Fazia, what have you done? What are you *doing*? How...?"

"Daddy, I'm so sorry, I'm so sorry... I can't hide it any longer. I know you'll hate me, but I can't help it."

"Fazia, you're my daughter – I love you. I could never hate you!"

As Fazia's attention was fully on her father, Dinah moved sideways behind a pillar and started to make her way around the edge of the concourse. She needed to get closer to Fazia, to be able to stop her if necessary. Subtle mental magic wasn't going to work now; it would have to be a direct attack.

"I'm a sorceress!" Tears slid down Fazia's cheeks. "I don't even know how it happened. I can't go back now – I'm infidel! And then those worms came, and those men died. I hate myself!"

Dinah crossed to the bottom of the now stationary escalator, but kept out of Fazia's line of sight. Wahid stood where he was, shocked. *Keep talking, keep talking,* Dinah thought.

"Fazia... daughter... It can't be true. We can talk to scholars, see what they say."

"Daddy, I've *read* the scholars! Everybody agrees, if a person practises magic, she can't be a Muslim! I looked *everywhere.* There isn't anything left for me." Fazia took a breath, then she spoke again. "I'm sorry, Daddy, I'm so sorry."

That was when Dinah felt it.

It wasn't as distinct as a tingle. It was more a sense of tension. Something had changed in the way power flowed through the world, as though a small plug had been taken out of a large bath; the water just starting to swirl.

She reached behind her back and took the Glock from its holster as she ran up the escalator.

Fazia turned to face her as she reached the top. The girl raised her hands, and Dinah felt the bridge starting to form. There was no time to check whether Faraday was in position; no time for a magical attack she hadn't prepared. She raised the gun and fired.

Crack.

Crack.

Crack.

The first and second bullets took Fazia in the chest. The third entered through the bridge of her nose and exited in a spray of blood and brain matter out of the back of her head.

The bridge spell dissipated as Fazia spun and slowly toppled over the edge of the mezzanine, tumbling through the broken barrier in a shower of shattered safety glass.

A second later, she hit the floor of the main concourse and lay still.

Wahid Ahmed's howl of grief broke the silence as he ran across the empty concourse, collapsed to his knees, and gathered his daughter's body into his arms.

Dinah lowered the gun and returned it to the holster. She walked across to the bloodstained glass where Fazia had fallen, then walked to the back of the mezzanine and sat down on the floor, her back against the wall, and rested her head on her knees.

A few minutes later, she heard the rustle of fabric and looked up to see Faraday sitting down beside her. He didn't say anything.

"I didn't know what else to do," she said.

Faraday said nothing.

"She was just a scared, confused kid, and I shot her." Dinah couldn't stop the tremor in her voice. "That could have been me. I was that out-of-control, only I got help instead of a bullet in the head."

Faraday said nothing.

Dinah felt tears welling up in her eyes, and wiped them away on her sleeve. "I didn't know what else to do. She was opening a bridge. I couldn't calm her down. I could have ripped her mind out by the roots, but she would have been just as dead. So I shot her. I don't even know where she was opening the bridge to – she could have been trying to escape."

Faraday said nothing.

"I know she killed a man – three, with the men in the tunnel. But that doesn't make it any better." Dinah dragged in a breath and scrubbed her sleeve over her face again. "I'm sorry, Kev. I'll get my shit together."

Dinah stood up and walked across to the edge of the mezzanine. Within hours, the glass would be repaired, the blood cleaned up. There would be no sign of what had happened. She would lead her team in destroying the remaining dholes, then she'd write a report and file it. And that would be the end of the matter: the team would move on to other threats, other missions.

But a girl was dead; a family destroyed. Would Wahid Ahmed ever recover from seeing his daughter shot dead in front of his eyes? Would he be able to keep working with people who thought his daughter a terrorist?

No, Dinah thought. *He won't.*

For a moment, she had a mental picture of invisible ripples of destruction moving outwards, slowly, inexorably. What would be the ultimate consequences of her actions today?

It was a question she couldn't afford to ask.

She took another deep breath. "All right. Back to work."

Faraday came up beside her. "That's the job, ma'am. You win some; you lose some. And some, even when you win, you lose."

---

*T.K. Elliott writes dark urban fantasy set in Birmingham, because she thinks what Birmingham needs is more eldritch horror. When not writing, she works in an office where there is a lot of coffee but not much magic. When not doing either of those things she flies a microlight aircraft, which doesn't include coffee but is pretty magical. Drop by her website at **tkelliott.com**, or say hello on Twitter (@t_k_elliott) or Goodreads.*

A Window Cracked

Guy Etchells

Monday, August 15th, 1977

He needed to find him. No matter what the evidence suggested or what the police concluded. He knew something wasn't right. He needed to find the truth before it was too late. He'd made a promise.

The old man watched as people went about their mundane daily tasks in New Street. He smiled, still fascinated by the culture of this time. Vibrant flowery shirts remained, but there were more fitted tops now. The hippie look had almost disappeared, replaced by cardigans, shirts with billowing sleeves, knee-high boots and platform shoes. Posters of Leo Sayer, Elvis Presley and Donna Summer filled a nearby shop window.

The old man's body tensed.

He felt a single sharp jolt, followed by an understanding that he'd been found and tagged. Hands tightened on his battered satchel. He strained his eyes and looked down towards Corporation Street.

With neither the place nor the need to hide, a dark figure that was decidedly different stepped out onto the pavement. The figure was much larger than any other on the street. It was no coincidence that the moment the old man had felt the jolt, the dark shadowy figure had turned slowly in his direction.

People seemed unaware of the macabre figure.

The old man found himself conflicted. He knew who the figure was but he couldn't leave, not without knowing the date. He looked around wildly, a cover of a magazine, a newspaper, anything. He raised his eyebrows and turned to the Odeon cinema, *Sinbad and the Eye of the Tiger*. Despite this small victory, he knew he was in big trouble: he'd been found. He narrowed his eyes; the people and New Street began to wash away.

Friday, March 16th, 2018

The rain had stopped but the streets were glassy with wetness. Birmingham city centre was holding its breath waiting for dawn still hours away. Except for the distant squeak of lorry brakes, all was peaceful.

The reflection shattered. The night sky, sombre buildings and shop windows. An array of neon lights and street lamps all washed together like a paintbrush swirled in clean water. The security guard exhaled and bent down to retrieve his keys from the puddle. He shook them, locked the final door on his round, and set the code on the keypad. He glanced at his watch: 1:34 a.m. He had only to walk to the car park and he'd be home in the warm in twenty minutes.

He zipped up his coat and watched a fox wander in front of the menswear store. It was about to turn down the side alley heading for New Street Station. It hesitated, mesmerised by the huge bull shimmering like Cara bronze ale in the city lights.

The security guard grinned. It wasn't the first time he'd seen the fox do this.

He walked towards the same alley and glanced to the right, down New Street, as he always did. He paused. An old man sat on one of the benches, facing down towards Corporation Street. It didn't feel right. Usually, he'd ignore the situation, not his problem and of course, there was the issue of safety. But the son in him argued that he couldn't ignore this. He'd never forgive himself if the old man needed help. Besides, he had a uniform and that carried a certain degree of weight.

"Excuse me, sir, are you okay?"

The old man looked up, shocked, then slightly annoyed, and returned his stare down New Street.

"My name's Theo, are you okay?" Theo noted that the old man was well dressed. "It's very late; you really shouldn't be out at this time alone."

Without altering his gaze, the old man fumbled in an aged leather satchel. He retrieved a tartan-patterned flask.

"Yes, yes. Everything's fine, thank you," he said. His eyes went back and forth over the dark shop fronts before they settled on a point close to the HSBC bank.

"Look, can I call someone? I mean... to come pick you up? Or I can get you a taxi?"

"No, I'm exactly where I need to be. I'll be on my way soon. Thank you."

Theo forced a smile. "Well if you're sure, I just don't like leaving an old man out here at this time. Lot o' loons out and about, you know."

The old man ignored him and shakily began to pour steaming coffee from his flask into a plastic cup.

Theo stepped away and pulled out his phone. He gave the local police station a ring.

"It's Theo from Bull Ring Security, I got an old gentleman down here, not the usual type. Bit worried he might be lost, or a bit mixed up, any chance you could... oh great, I'll stay with him, till they get here." Moments later, he sat gently beside the old man.

"I'm sure someone's worried about you. Are you waiting for someone?"

The old man breathed out. His shoulders dropped. He looked at Theo and then chuckled. "Yes, yes. I am waiting for someone and quite frankly, I'm getting a little tired of it."

"How long?" Theo asked, smiling back. "How long have you been waiting?"

"Forty-one years," answered the old man.

Wednesday, April 4ᵗʰ, 2018

Inside the bookstore, David snatched the large bunch of keys off Till Three and headed towards the front doors. Ella hurried behind him, trying to keep up.

"Are all the tills done?" he asked.

"They am," Ella replied breathlessly. "Did 'em first thing. Left Till Four empty thou, no point unless it gets busy."

David turned the key in the lock and the grille started to ascend. "What time did you spot it?"

"I walked past at 8.10, but it wor there at seven. I would a noticed it. Did you hear anything?"

"No, not a thing."

They walked out onto New Street and turned to look at the left store window. A large crack bled its way up. David rubbed his hands over his face.

"How the hell could this have happened?" He bent down and examined the fracture.

Ella looked across at the Odeon cinema and down to HSBC.

"Well, it's only glass, ay it!" She wrapped her arms around her chest. "Maybe someone kicked it, or didn't I hear that temperatures can bust glass?"

David got up and shook his head. "It's not toughened glass like you'd think; they only use that on smaller windows. Thanks to those flamin' riots in 2011, head office decided all the flag stores should get adequate protection."

"That was all the lootings we saw in London and stuff?"

"Yeah."

"Flamin' crazy days them was."

"Huge risk assessment went ahead and we, my dear, got replacements of very thick laminated glass," he grinned. "Interlayered sheets of glass if you really want to know."

Ella dropped her arms. "You sat up and read about it, didn't you?"

David smirked and took another look at the crack. "Nah, just wanted to impress the boss back then. I doubt a kick would cause this." He blew out slowly, looking up and down the street. "Head office ain't gonna like this," he said in a Texas accent that he knew would make Ella smile. "Wait a sec, how long's that man been sat there?"

Ella glanced at an old man sitting on one of the benches opposite the store. "Oh, he's bin there all morning."

"Can you sort the staff breaks for me?"

"Sure."

David headed over to the old man.

"Good morning, sir."

He was well-dressed with winter-white hair and a gentle face.

The old man looked up and smiled. "Not often you get a good morning nowadays."

"I'm sorry to bother you; I'm the manager, well... acting manager of the store here." He pointed. "Have you seen anyone by the front of the store in the last hour or so?"

"By the window? Um, no I don't think I have."

"Anyone stop, or a loud noise maybe?"

"No, I'm sorry. Is it to do with that broken window?"

"Yes... it is."

The old man laughed politely. "I'm very sorry. I haven't been paying much attention."

"I can understand that; it's a beautiful morning."

"Yes, yes, it is."

David hesitated and glanced around. "You know, I've worked here for nearly two years. I still forget there are trees in New Street."

"Sycamores," the old man said. "Yes, it's true, but then we don't see what's in front of us half the time, do we? Well, maybe we do... when it's gone."

"That's true."

"Did you know New Street was built to be the Bond Street of Birmingham?"

"No. No, I didn't." David looked at this watch. "Okay, I'd better go, opening up in fifteen, need to rally the troops. Thanks anyway and have a good day."

"Oh, I'm sorry I couldn't help you with the window."

David paused. "So, are you waiting for someone?"

"Oh no," the old man answered, a crack in his voice. "I just like to sit and watch the world go by and solve mysteries in my head."

David noticed Ella waving at him from the store entrance.

"Sounds a great way to spend a day."

"Oh, my father used to think so too," the old man began, arching a sly brow. "He was a bit superstitious you know. He believed, when a window cracked, it was an omen or something..."

"Something bad?" David interrupted.

"No! No, not all the time. Good also."

"Not sure head office will see it that way. Oh well, if you do remember anything..."

The old man held out his hand. "Mr Halford, like the shop, George Halford."

"Mr Halford. If you do remember anything just pop into the bookstore and ask for Dave." He gave Mr Halford a warm smile. "Thanks again." David headed into the store.

Mr Halford took out a notebook and pen and resumed his stare down New Street.

Thursday, April 5th, 2018

"I'm off out to get a sandwich while it's quiet." David held out the store keys to Ella, who saluted at him over Till Three.

"That old bugger's still thea," she said and nodded towards the entrance.

"Who?"

"The old bloke yesterday, sat outside. Still thea."

"Is he?"

"You think he's all right? Maybe he's just soft in the head or something."

"He seemed okay."

"Arrrh, it's a shame, ah it."

"If Theo from security pops his head in, mention it, will you?"

Ella frowned "Which one's Theo?"

"The one you keep ogling."

"Oh, you mean the ginger one? Ar, he's bostin, he is."

"That's the one."

Coffees and sandwiches clutched to his chest, David navigated through a sea of bodies, past Marks & Spencer's and up High Street. Turning right at the Rotunda, his gaze fell upon Mr Halford.

"Hello again, Mr Halford, you still here?"

Mr Halford smiled. "Um? Oh, hello. Oh yes, yes. I'm not entirely sure I'm finished here yet."

David sat down. He struggled to balance the coffees and sandwiches. "I have to ask you, what exactly are you doing?"

"Told you yesterday; solving a mystery."

"What mystery, Mr Halford?"

"It's George, call me George."

"Okay, George."

"Well, you see, I've always loved mysteries, especially those that were never solved. Since I retired and lost my dear wife, I've been researching old mysteries."

"That sounds great. I'd love mysteries and I'm mad on local history, I've made a great section in the store, I may even write about it one day."

"Aarh now, there's one mystery I need to solve before... well," he fumbled with his satchel, "before I get too old to get out of the house. It was a mystery my wife wanted solving before she passed."

"Sounds good, George."

"In April 1978 a teenager named Matthew from Walsall was found dead. Believed murdered, right here in New Street, after a night out with friends. They never found who did it."

"Never?"

George shook his head. "Never! Multiple head injuries consistent with being hit with a blunt object, they reported." George pointed. "Poor lad was left to die, alone just over there."

David looked up the street. It was unsettling to know that people happily shopped where a young man had lost his life.

"What about DNA evidence? Oh, wait! There wasn't DNA back then was there?" David felt a little embarrassed.

"No," George replied. "Nothing like that back then."

"So, they never found who did it?" asked David.

"Not to this day. I did read that another person was attacked in Cheapside, Digbeth on the very same night but survived. They had head injuries too, but they couldn't remember who'd attacked them, to traumatised."

"Mysteries, eh?"

"Indeed."

David took a swig of one of the coffees. He screwed up his face. It wasn't particularly hot. "So how are you going to solve this mystery, George?"

George smiled cheekily, and it was then that David realised George Halford wasn't in any way mentally ill, delusional or an idiot.

"More importantly, have you solved the mystery of your shop window?"

David shrugged. "Think that's going to remain a mystery too. The new manager can solve it, whoever that'll be."

"Thought you were the manager?"

"Acting manager. The role's being advertised."

"Are you applying for it?"

"Yes, definitely." David jabbed his finger at the store. "I've worked in that store two years. It's the best store out the lot of 'em. The company can send me anywhere, but it's here in Birmingham where I wanna be."

George beamed "My wife used to say, home is wherever you happen to be."

"Yeah, I get that, but... I'm struggling to find a reason to get up every morning, knowing that... well, I may not get the position. I actually consider it my store, daft as that sounds. I've built up a core of local writers and their fans. It's a dream, I know, but a dream worth chasing, a goal, a purpose."

"Well," George scoffed. "They're fools not to give you the job."

"I know," David said. He glanced down at the sandwiches and coffee. "Oh well, I'd better get these back."

"Okay lad, don't work too hard."

David rose. "My dad always says that but now I always do too," he laughed. "See you, George."

Sunday, April 9th, 2018

The next few days were busy at the bookstore. Staff off sick meant longer hours without proper breaks. David noticed George sitting on the bench, eyes fixed down New Street, but it wasn't until Sunday afternoon that it was quiet enough for David to step out.

"Hey, George, how's the mystery solving going?"

"Oh, afternoon, son, come on, sit down." George moved his flask and foil wrapped sandwiches.

"Thanks."

"I'm getting fairly close, I'd say. I see your window's still broken."

"Yeah. Being done early tomorrow morning."

"Oh, that's good then. And the job, what's happening there?" George asked.

"Interview's in London, Tuesday afternoon."

"Sorted then," George smiled. "You'll be fine."

They both sat in silence for a moment. The shoppers swerved and dodged each other like bumper cars.

"George, tell me, how will you solve the mystery of that lad in 1978 by sitting here every day?"

"And some nights," George added, drumming his fingers on his satchel.

David turned to George. "Nights too?"

A cold breeze blew down the street. It stirred the sycamores' newly emerging leaves, causing the shoppers to pause and look around.

"Do you trust me, David?" George asked.

"Erm... I don't really know you."

"You're a good lad, though."

David shook his head and smirked. "Nah! I wouldn't exactly call me a lad now."

"Well, you're a lad to someone as old as me," George laughed. "But I've seen you, over there, working in that store."

David tensed up. "Should I be worried?"

"No, don't be silly, but the way you treat the public, your staff and that Black Country lass..."

"Oh, that's Ella, she's just applied for management training."

"Probably inspired by you."

David smiled and glanced down at his shoes.

"Ella, she looks up to you."

"She's a bobby dazzler that one."

"Eh!" George cried. "That's a real Black Country saying!"

"So, George, you can see all that by just sitting here?"

"I see what needs to be seen." He unwrapped a cheese and onion sandwich. "I know you all think I'm a stupid old man, sitting here, doing this, day in, day out..."

"I don't think you're stupid, George."

"But really, I am doing what I say I am." He gathered his collar around his neck. "Time to go down the rabbit hole, Alice," he muttered.

"Eh?"

"Lewis Carroll." George pointed down New Street. "What do you see?"

David looked down passed the Odeon cinema. Past the Burlington Hotel, Primark, O2, The Works. Further on, to the little stalls and down to Corporation Street and the ramp where a musician played the saxophone.

He watched crowds move, in and out like a beach tide. Phones pinned to their ears. Heads bent down subservient to their hand-held masters.

They abruptly all stopped.

Silence came, no music, no bustle, nothing.

The people began to wash away and the scene around him changed.

Kate Bush's '*Wuthering Heights*' erupted from a shop. It competed with Blondie's '*Denis*' lower down the street. It was the overriding noise and the smell of traffic that dominated David's senses. The Odeon was still the cinema; however, the Burlington was now the Midland Hotel. New Street was manic. Cars, buses, and people swarmed everywhere. Newspapers had one of two words, 'IRA' or 'Thatcher', splashed across the front page. A group of children dressed in coloured tank-tops, zip-up cardigans and flared shirts, were in awe of a poster of *Starsky & Hutch* in *Look-in* magazine. Adults dressed in flares, platforms, fringes, and suede. Women looked like a mix between Joni Mitchell and Cher and every man looked like an Osmond brother. Punks highlighted the scene with their hair dyed bright colours, wearing torn sleeveless t-shirts, military boots, and confidence. *Saturday Night Fever* had left its impact as clones of John Travolta's Tony Manero strutted past.

The bench they sat upon was slap-bang, on the road. No pedestrianised area existed, just pavements gorged with shoppers. Cream and navy buses weaved their way up and down the street, with Minis, Ford Escorts, Capris and an Austin Princess.

The vehicles disappeared as they approached, only to appear behind them a second later.

David gasped. He glanced at George, then back again. The people vanished, and the scene changed once again. Everything was back to the way it was.

People quickly passed David, looking down at him a mixture of fear and concern in their expressions.

George put a gentle hand on his shoulder.

"I think you'd better close your mouth, son."

"But that was... how did you.... are you telling me you can see through time?"

"Just tell me what you're thinking, David."

"I'm thinking hallucinogens, drugs, flash mobs, TV set-up."

"None of them."

"But how?"

"I don't know how. Only, that I can."

"I can't... I just don't believe it," David gasped for a second time. "That isn't... normal." The word sounded funny, as though he knew that normal was a word that would never really apply to him again.

"I see it as peeking through time, like watching TV," George said. "Do you know, I caught the end of the pub bombings in 74... horrific!"

"This is incredible!"

George calmly took a bite out of his sandwich. "I see it as a gift, nothing more."

David tried to speak. His eyes flitted around the street. He stood up, despair flooding him.

"I'm not comfortable with this." Without a single look at George, he ran into the store.

Saturday, April 8th, 1978

The dark figure saw the old man and the bench appear with someone new. It ignored the swirling chaos of New Street and continued to stagger. As long as the old man was here, it could move. Its movements were inhumanly slow and painful, but it did not waver in its course or new objective.

It headed forward.

The old man suddenly vanished and the figure stopped.

It would wait.

Tuesday, April 10th, 2018

Aside from the January sales, the store had just had its busiest weekend of the year, so far. David was glad he hadn't the time to think about what he'd witnessed on Sunday with George.

Tuesday had come and David travelled down to London, nervous and excited. This would be his biggest ever interview.

Late that afternoon, he got on the London Euston 17.43 direct to Birmingham. He had Wednesday off, and with the interview now over, he was trapped in a carriage for 1 hour 22 mins. There was little option but to reflect and ponder.

Thursday, April 12th, 2018

April showers began in earnest. Cold days remained, and the wind blew in. It brought heavy clouds that sprinkled drizzle on the heads of people in New Street.

At 10.55 the rain ceased. The sun seeped down through the clouds, striking the street with pools of soft golden light.

David sat on the bench and offered George a coffee. There, they sat in silence, watching the lazy clouds and the leaves on the sycamores drinking in the sunlight. They listened to the chatter of the people and found it comforting and familiar.

"Did you know, the Bull Ring Bull weighs about six tonnes?" George asked at last.

"No," replied David. "But I know it was placed there in 2003."

"2003? That long ago?"

"Yep. Time flies."

"Is it really made of bronze?"

David smiled. "Yes, it is."

They sat there observing more people emerge onto both High Street and New Street.

"You can always tell the office workers." George indicated, leaning forward. "They always wear black, like ants flooding out of a nest to face an intruder."

"You noticed that too?" David laughed. "It's the 11.00 coffee run before lunch."

"How did the interview go?"

"Not a clue." David offered a vague smile. "Feel it went as good as it could. Other candidates, well... I think they had a little more experience in management roles. They asked some pretty tricky questions." He took a swig of coffee. "George, does anyone else know... about what you can do?"

"My wife," replied George. "It took a bit of convincing, I can tell you. I don't think she ever forgave me or really understood, Bless her."

"How long have you... you know, been able to see through time?"

"Quite a few years."

"And, can you be anywhere? I mean, could you be in another city or country, like Cyprus or Willenhall, and see back in time."

"Frankly, I don't really know." He cocked his head. "However, I do know that it seems to work better when I've an emotional connection to a place. You yourself said that you love this city, this street in particular, and that store."

"Yes."

"Which is why it made it easier to show you." He ran his fingers over his chin. "Very easy in fact. I tried to do some research once and settled on the assumption that peeking attaches to both the emotional and memory centres of the brain."

"But George, how are you going to solve the mystery about a teen from 1978 by just... watching?"

"Because I've done it before. I'm not trying to solve it... not really. I just need to know, was he murdered? Did he die alone?"

"So, you're sort of... hooked, like my mom is? She's always watching soaps. She can't miss a single episode."

George gave David a comical glare. "As I sit here, events move in 1978 almost at a similar pace. I've been waiting for April 1978, and a particular Saturday night."

David considered. "Where did this gift come from?"

"I don't know much but... my father passed the gift on to me. He received it from his mother and she got it from her nanny back during the war."

David's eyes widened "So, it's not passed down genetically then?"

"No, not biological at all, it appears. I was surprised to find that, too. It reminds me of those who deal in magic and how they can pass a spell to a loved one, such as a protection spell. Shaman, warlocks, mages do it; maybe it's something like that. It may just be all nonsense, I don't understand it really, but perhaps we're not supposed to. Sometimes we just have to take things on faith."

"But what's the point of waiting, and watching though? It's not like you go to the police if you see who the killer of this boy is."

"I'm near now," George turned away. "Extremely close to solving this. I simply can't miss it. I'll never have the chance again."

"Are you... you know, doing it now, looking?"

"Peeking." George smiled and turned back.

"Okay, peeking, back to 1978?"

"No, I can... what is it you say these days, zone in, and out?" His eyes moved over David's face.

It wasn't much, but David felt a small surge of sadness.

101

George looked away and fiddled with his coffee lid. "I sometimes get afraid, that if I fall asleep, I'll miss the actual event I'm searching for." He took a deep breath. "There's something else, David. My father back then warned me that there are figures. Creatures locked away in time, evil things, drifters. They can't be seen by those existing in real time. They are weak, almost frozen in time. But they are mindful and drawn to those who shouldn't be there. If you happen to be around and not in your own time, they'll spot you..." George spread his hands wide. "Let's just say they'll never stop looking for you."

David responded with an exaggerated shake of his head. "I guess there had to be a downside. Where do they come from?"

"I don't know. The more you use the gift in a particular period then... the closer they appear to get." George's tone turned serious. "It feels like they lock on to you."

David forced a laugh. "I'm still struggling just believing all this. Have you ever seen one of these... figures?"

George smiled afresh and looked away. "No, no. Guess I've been lucky."

"Can you show me again, George? Take a gander... peeking? I think I'm ready now."

Thursday, April 13th, 1978

The scene changed. George turned to the dark distant figure and inhaled sharply. The figure had crossed over Corporation Street. Although inexorable, the figure was moving slowly closer. In a matter of months, it had managed to push its way nearer.

George had counted a hundred and ninety-four steps from the bench to where Corporation Street crossed New Street. They both seemed fixed on each other despite the distance, too far to see any expression, but George already knew the figure had no face.

Predator and prey, each fully aware of each other's status. The grim figure continued to stare at him with unwavering authority.

George felt an wave of desperation and hunger emanating from the creature. His skin began to tingle, his heart raced. Then a voice hissed inside his head. It sounded human but distorted, irregular and evil.

"*You know what I'm coming for. You know what I want.*"

Tuesday, April 17th, 2018

David stood over George and gestured over his shoulder with his thumb.

"You're looking at the new manager of that store."

George looked up, with a frown.

David waited for the penny to drop.

"You got the job?" George cried out.

"Yep!"

"That's fantastic news!" He rose and shook David's hand. "I can see you're going to be fine. Oh, what wonderful news!"

David fell onto the bench with a sigh.

"I honestly thought the area manager was visiting to tell me I hadn't got it." David smiled indulgently. "No second interview needed. They want me to run the Birmingham store, effective immediately."

"But you didn't think you had a chance, lad, you said the others had more experience."

"They may have, but they want to take the stores in a slightly new direction," he spread his hands into the air. "Expanding the range, attracting a new, younger market. They really liked my presentation and vision for the store. Bringing in events, and the local community. Since I've been an acting manager, targets have been met, and the store's performing well, and staff are... well, they're happy."

David grinned and leaned forward, elbows on his knees. "I can't believe it. A few weeks ago, I felt pretty uncertain about things."

George held out a white paper bag. "I didn't bring anything to celebrate. So, boiled sweets will have to do. What did Ella and the staff say? Will there be some sort of celebration, do you think?"

David cautiously peered behind him, like a naughty child.

"Nah! I haven't told them yet. I put on a sad face, and said I was taking a break."

George waggled his index finger and gave a loud tut-tut.

"You're very bad. But I'm honoured you chose to tell me first... I'm quite touched. Thank you, David."

Wednesday, April 18th, 2018

The next morning, before the store opened, David received a text from Ella, as he sat in the office. He thought it odd, as she was already in the store.

He ran down the stairs and through the door to the shop floor. Normally, he would shout to the team 'everything ready for opening?' but the store was uninhabited. He grinned and sauntered to the already open storefront.

He'd told the staff that he'd been appointed as the manager the night before. To say they were thrilled and animated was an understatement.

He stepped out to the sound of cheering and looked at Ella, George and the rest of his staff with a huge smile and red face. He swaggered over, much to the delight of the staff. This had now attracted the attention of passersby who thought it was some kind of happy fire drill.

"What are you like?" he shouted. "This isn't a TV reality show." They all laughed. "Guess I'm going to get sod all work out of you today then?"

Ella appeared with a cake. The word 'BOSS' was iced across the top. David laughed and clapped his hands. "Thanks, everyone, but come on, we open up in twenty minutes, get your asses in there, and get off the street, you're embarrassing me."

The staff chatted happily as they filtered back into the store. Ella steered David onto the bench next to George and they all sat down. Ella nodded to George who revealed a small speaker and shakily pressed a button on his mobile. Etta James' '*At Last*,' played out. Office and retail workers passed by and tried not to smile.

David couldn't say much, he just grinned and glanced from Ella to George.

"Well, you and the store..." George shrugged his shoulders. "Well, it's like a love story, and now it's yours... at last."

David and Ella cracked up and there they sat, staring down New Street listening to Etta James vocals. Their eyes rolled skyward as the clouds parted and the sun once again shone down.

Saturday, April 28th, 2018

It was the end of April and another Saturday. The rain clouds gathered more and more and the days became grey and wet. George was not deterred. He unwrapped his cheese and onion sandwiches from their foil coat and unscrewed the plastic cup from his flask. His hands worked automatically with routine and experience, while he continuously watched. He'd got up earlier than normal that morning and caught the 529 bus with a nasty sense of foreboding.

By the afternoon, the street was saturated with people finding distraction from the weather by shopping and socialising. George hardly left the bench, and when he did he returned to find it taken. He stood beneath one of the sycamores and watched a street band playing in the rain.

Evening came; thunder rumbled over the city and the streets began to clear. Darkness crept in and cold air tickled his skin. Coatless girls with bare arms and short skirts tiptoed around puddles, laughing. Lads on a stag night followed close behind. As the Midland Metro hummed past Corporation Street, George pulled his coat collar high around his neck and focussed.

New Street faded away, the scene shifted, and he saw the street darken. People poured out of The Odeon. Women shrieked at the rain, fumbling with umbrellas, and transparent plastic headscarves. Others hung around poster boards promoting *Tomorrow Never Comes*, starring Oliver Reed, and Susan George; there were even early promotions for films called *Grease* and *Jaws 2*. The traffic still raced up and down, the rain just made it all appear more chaotic.

George became anxious as he watched. 1978 was no different than being in the present; just fashion and ethnicities were different. It almost seemed fundamentally wrong how similar it all was.

George searched the scene of a wet 1978 New Street with panic on his face. Lights sparkled, on the surfaces of puddles, only to be smashed apart by more rain.

The people and the traffic in the street began to disperse.

"This is it," he muttered. "This is the night he gets killed... I'm here, I'll know the truth." Trembling, he tucked his hands into his pockets and stared into the dark knowing the whole time he was being watched.

As midnight approached, he stood up. Unsteadily, he took a few steps forward, and watched as a pale, thin teen with curly brown hair, dressed in a corduroy brown jacket, bell bottom jeans and trainers, walked up New Street. The young man stopped in a shop doorway at the side of the Odeon, to avoid the rain. He kicked a can and began to light up. The flame of the cigarette lighter revealed his face and George drew a breath.

It was Matthew.

He'd found him.

Matthew rubbed his temples and kept his head down. He moved, from one foot to the other, and blew into his hands. He finally stopped and peered down the street.

George could hardly breathe.

In the distance, music could be heard, laughter, and shouting. The sound of traffic, the squeaking brakes of buses. Somehow, a city still had the ability to make one feel so alone and helpless. George's eyes filled and his lips trembled as he stood watching the young man, calmly smoking, waiting.

George sensed another presence. He spun around. Someone had appeared behind him, further down the street by the Rotunda.

Matthew was facing the opposite way so wouldn't see him.

This new man crept forward, keeping to the shadows. He dodged swiftly into shop doors to avoid detection.

George wanted to call out, warn Matthew, but he panicked and stumbled back to the bench. "What was I thinking? I can't watch him die, not him."

The stranger was almost upon Matthew. He was so close now. Suddenly, the stranger ran forward throwing himself at Matthew. George covered his face.

He heard Matthew scream. Then, laugh.

"Hey loser, so got you that time!"

George uncovered his face, to see the stranger piggybacking on Matthew who spun around and threw him off against the wall.

"Fuck's sake, Tach! Don't do that, you scared the shit out of me!"

"Yeah, yeah, quit your crying."

George held his fist to his mouth as he listened to Matthew's voice. He watched, He watched and tried to hear what they were talking about.

Tach took a cigarette, slapped Matthew on the arm, said goodbye and headed off down New Street.

It began to rain more heavily. Matthew looked around and decided to shelter in one of the red telephone boxes. There, he lit another cigarette.

A group ran down passed him laughing, crossing over from Millets to Peter Lord's then continuing passed the taxi ranks. They screamed in the rain, like children. Someone shouted something, and they all changed direction like a flock of birds and headed over to the ramp at the side of the Midland Bank.

"*You know what I want.*"

The voice sounded in his head, unmistakable, controlled and sinister.

"I thought I'd have more time," George muttered, looking up at the tall dark figure standing beside him. There were no features, just a swirling of shadows in the shape of a man.

A dark hand extended towards George and long gnarled fingers wrapped gently around his delicate throat.

George swallowed. "I've heard stories about your kind," he said. "I know I'll never be free from you."

"*I've been waiting... for you... a long time.*" The figure growled.

George stiffened. "I'm just an old man with very little life left to give. You must need my gift, my ability."

"*Yes. With it, I can escape this place.*"

George found himself smiling. "I'm only here, now, because a host such as me can still contain just enough of the gift for a few days more after he's passed it on," he paused. "Yes, you heard right, I'm just an echo now, an echo of the power you want. You're too late! You're too late!" George stared up at the figure, gasping. "The gift has been passed to another and you will never leave this place," he closed his eyes and readied himself. "You're a monster! My father taught me well, and I will not be intimidated by you!"

He found that he could not move. His heart pounded, and his lungs heaved.

"*Then, I shall take that which is most valuable to you.*"

George felt cold fingers leave his throat.

"*Your remaining time.*" The voice hissed.

He opened his eyes.

There was a shifting movement of light and the shadow figure was gone.

George felt his neck and calmed himself. He turned his attention to the sound of banging. Where was it coming from? The telephone box, it had steamed up. George watched in paralysed horror, as a head hit the tiny windows and frames of the phone box. He almost felt the impact, as Matthew's head was slammed into the frame repeatedly.

It was all over in seconds.

Matthew emerged, staggering out of the box. Blood poured down his head and covered his coat. He spun and slammed his head into the open door of the phone box. Disorientated, he fell backwards and smashed into a street lamp. He collapsed to the ground, convulsing in the rain till at last, he lay motionless.

George watched paralysed.

A man, in sodden tattered denim, sprinted up from Corporation Street, floundering through the deluge. He constantly looked back, over his shoulder.

He shrieked as he almost fell over Matthew's body and threw himself against the wall.

A metal object left his hand and fell to the floor. It made a loud clang, then a ringing sound. The man scrambled to regain his footing. Looking frantically at both the body, and back down the street, he then ran on, up New Street smashing through puddles, sprinting towards the market area, and into darkness.

George didn't know how long he waited. All sense of time disappeared. He watched immobilised, as a young woman with an umbrella, passed by. She dropped her bags and was on the floor in seconds holding Matthew's head. George couldn't hear her words, he just caught the word *Rosemary*, but she was talking gently to him, stroking his hair. He was touched by this woman. Someone he'd never seen before, just a stranger, on her way home. But here she was, holding the young man's body in the rain.

People then appeared everywhere.

"Call an ambulance!"

The woman stayed until the sound of sirens came. Then, she was consumed by the crowd and disappeared.

"George? George?" The world spun and morphed back to modern day. George, looked up to see several people looking at him as he knelt in the rain. A police car and ambulance, with lights flashing stood nearby.

A security guard knelt down next to him in the puddle with his arm firmly around him. "George, George mate, it's me."

George recognised him and examined the face blinking tears from bloodshot eyes. It was Theo the security guard.

"He wasn't murdered," George said to him. "No one killed him," his voice began to crack. "It was a fit or seizure... he didn't die alone, he didn't die alone." George broke down and fell into Theo's arms.

Friday, May 11th, 2018

Another long and busy week passed for David. It was unusual to see other people sat on the bench throughout the day, and then empty in the evening. He should have taken George's number. Nearly ten days had passed.

He was sitting in his office alone, sorting the holiday rotas, when the window cracked.

He got up and walked over, remembering what George had said. A window cracked when something good happened. Hadn't that been the day he'd met George? Was this also a sign? David looked beyond the window, down to the street. He quickly strode out his office, and down to the shop floor. He passed Ella putting stock out on shelves.

"You okay?" She asked. "Post's arrived. I'll put it in your office, do you want me to..."

He cut her off with a raised hand.

"I'll be right back," he said and rushed out of the store.

The security guard paused outside Pizza Hut, turning his head, hearing his name.

"Morning, Dave."

"Hey, Theo."

"Ella told me you got the manager post, congratulations."

"Yeah, cheers, mate. I erm... do you, or have you seen the old guy, who's been sitting on the bench outside the store?"

"You mean George?"

"Yeah, George, George Halford." David raised his eyebrows. Theo knew him by name.

"Dave, I'm sorry. George passed away a week ago. If I'd known you were a friend, I'd have let you know." Theo watched the lost expression on David's face. "Shit! Sorry mate. I met him, back in March," Theo continued. "It was really late when I was locking up. I always gave him a lift back home after my shift, most nights... you know, to make sure the old fellow got home safe. Not really sure what he was up to... guessing he was a bit lonely."

"He was erm, solving a mystery," David whispered. "Trying to find out who'd killed this teenager, Matthew, back in the 70s."

"Yeah, that's the one," Theo continued. "He told me how Matthew was supposedly killed in 1978, but the killer had never been caught. The case was never really closed and George and his wife couldn't move on. Can't imagine losing your child like that."

"Matthew was his son?" Now it all made sense, Matthew being George's son and the promise George made to his wife.

111

"Yeah, when I last spoke to him, he was convinced that Matthew died of some brain thingy, or some kind of fit, and his injuries, only looked like an attack."

"But there had already been an attack, on another guy in Digbeth, with some metal object or something hadn't there?"

"Yeah, a pipe was found near Matthew's body. Rain washed away a lot of evidence; we are talking the 70s here. George's said that a guy had run all the way from Digbeth, with the pipe he'd used to kill with. Guess he was hoping to stash it away far from the scene. He stumbled across Matthew's body, here in New Street. Panicked more, dropped it, and legged it. Weird thing is," Theo muttered, "George was really happy about it. Kept saying his son hadn't died alone, that someone had sat with him. I think he was getting a bit mixed up. I found him here, some kind of breakdown, the hospital said. Poor bugger."

Saturday, May 12th, 2018

David slowly raised his face toward the office ceiling and closed his eyes as tightly as he could. So, George had found, and then watched Matthew, his son, die. He had seen what really happened on that night. Tears squeezed under his eyelids and rolled down his cheeks. His chest felt heavy. Finally, he opened his eyes again. He could barely see through his tears. An envelope lay in front of him. He opened it.

The letter was beautifully handwritten.

Dear David.

I can't tell you how much I have enjoyed sitting and talking with you these past weeks. Meeting you was something, very special.

I knew that once I had discovered the truth about Matthew's death, no matter what it was, I would be able to let go. I had promised that to my wife, and now, I can rest and be with her.

You reminded me, so very much of what's it's like to have a son again, even if only for a brief time.

The day the window cracked was indeed a good sign, David, because it brought you to me, a sign that it was time to pass on a gift. Enjoy it, use it and love it as I have done.

Be happy and thank you.

George. J. Halford.

Monday, May 14th, 2018

David sat, silent on the bench, his hands folded around his coffee. He watched the movement of the people around him. The huge sadness that had rolled down on him suddenly didn't feel so heavy anymore. To anyone who saw him, he just looked like a young man, content, someone who liked to watch and listen to the sounds of the city.

He spied Ella. She glanced at him, through the store window. She smiled, and he winked back.

He turned his attention down New Street and watched as the Birmingham crowds began to wash away and the scene around him change.

It was summer, and the day was warm. New Street was bathed in yellows and golds. People swarmed about, wearing torn denim and big hair, crimped Mohawks and mullets; groups of girls, dressed like Madonna and Bananarama. The men were clones of George Michael, Limahl and Simon Le Bon. He looked across at the Odeon. A huge grin slowly emerged, and he wanted to laugh. *National Lampoon's Vacation* and *Return of the Jedi* were being shown. He tilted his head to the side. In the distance, up on High Street David could hear Ultravox's *Vienna*.

He smiled.

"Thank you, George. I will."

Guy Etchells is a teacher, writer and keen gardener living in Birmingham. Born and raised in the Black Country, Guy is a graduate of the MA in Writing at Birmingham City University: he won first prize in Scripting and Staging for his play Four Men One Pub. *His debut novel,* The Cubicle at the End, *an urban paranormal mystery, is out in 2019.*

The Six That Matches the Twelve

Nicky Tate

Everyone said pregnancy suited Perl, although Josek wasn't sure he agreed. He missed her make-up and glossy leather high-heeled shoes. When they'd arrived in Erdington, two years past, back in the Spring of '81, she'd been in her element. From their early courtship in Gdansk she'd always been immaculately turned out, even when they had precious little. Here with a *Boots* on the High Street offering a colourful battery of cosmetics – well! – she blossomed. He would find all sorts in the bathroom; palettes of neon pink and blue eyeshadow, bean scrubs and curious bronzing balls in a tub of pinky-brown dust. Josek had a spring in his step with this tall slim blonde on his arm. He'd preened once, when he overheard a teenage boy talking to his mate on the bus.

"She's a fucking ten mate. That's what I want."

Perl received the news that they were expecting when business was brisk. The café had just got its new neon sign. He remembered waking, and coming downstairs to hear her already up and about in the red butterfly dressing gown, putting washing on the line at five in the morning. When he had asked her what the hell she was doing she said she was so happy that she just couldn't sleep. He laughed and made some tea and together they sat on the garden step, with the wind fluttering her robe.

Now just a month remained before the baby was due. Perl was seated, fat and open-legged on the cork tiles in the kitchen. The square plastic washing up bowl alongside her, she wiped and scrubbed the insides of the cupboards as if she wanted to scrape the surfaces away.

115

She'd given up on the make-up after it had begun to make her itch, and lost the lightness as the bump became startlingly large; and she'd complained that her hips constantly ached although there was nothing the doctor could do, or even prescribe, because of the baby.

She'd had her hair cut the previous week – her beautiful long, blonde hair now cropped into a fluffy, flicky sort of style. She said she wanted to look like Princess Di. Privately, Josek found it called to mind the back end of a chicken. Now and then he felt the gloomy sense of an ending.

The evicted pans and tins teetered in a ziggurat on the kitchen surface. Josek attempted to arrange them into a less precarious configuration as he fought his way to the kettle.

"And that lot need binning, Every single one. I want it all new, Josek."

"Whatever you say sweetheart." Josek lifted the trays to examine them. In fairness, they were, largely, poorly-made. Those they had bought in the UK were as thin as tin cans, flimsy with no weight at all to them. No wonder they had buckled and the handles had come loose from the pots, although admittedly Perl treated kitchen utensils like hammers. The old tins from Poland were solid, even if blackened with age.

He gathered the British crap from the pile and threw them into a cardboard box. The weightier Polish relics would stay, he decided. Perl had shoved them in her bin pile but Josek retrieved them and slid them back in the cupboard.

"I'll take them to the tip. I can go up Rackhams and get some new. Is this rubbish too?"

He grasped a pile of thin brochures by the kettle.

"No! Leave them. They're from the college." Perl stood uneasily and grabbed them from him, carrying them into the living room and placing them on a high shelf. "They do English language. I'm sick of the Saturday girls laughing at me."

"No one's laughing at you, sweetheart. Your English is fine."

"Well, it would be nice to swear at them in their own language."

"Come on, that's not fair, they're only kids. But how would that work anyway – in classroom with the baby?"

"See? I was worried about that, but the brochure says they have a crèche."

"What the fuck is a crèche?"

Perl flicked her hand at Josek and stomped back off to the kitchen.

He shouted at her back. "I'm not criticising darling, I just don't see why you can't relax and enjoy just being with the baby?"

Drawers were opening and slamming. "I already feel trapped, Josek. I'm stuck in this bloody house and I'll be stuck here with the baby too. I am going to go mad."

"There's always the café. You'll meet plenty of people there."

Something else was slammed. "Oh yes! I'll get to have wonderful conversations! Belly Buster or just the Big Breakfast? One or two sugars in your tea?"

She came back into the room, tearful now. He pulled her into a hug and they embraced as best they could around her bump. She was cold and tense, and after sobbing thoroughly, she sniffed and collected herself.

"Maybe I'll go and stay with Donna for a few days? I can get the train."

Josek wasn't keen on Donna. She was a gregarious girl who had lodged with them during their first year. She and Perl had been close, for a time, and he was grateful that she'd eased his wife's transition into British life. Donna was rude and spiteful about people, however, and although her anecdotes caused Perl to howl with laughter, Josek felt a visceral repulsion. Still, he reasoned, as long as he didn't have to go and visit the flat-chested bore, it was fine by him.

Perl seemed to remember something; her tone changed, "Oh! But it's our anniversary this weekend and I wanted us to do something special together."

Josek had forgotten this fact entirely. "Sweetheart, we have many more anniversaries together; like you say, you need a change of scenery. Go and have fun, have a few drinks and a laugh. That would make me happy."

Perl's face softened and, smiling, she nodded and wiped her eyes on a tea-towel.

"Thanks, sweetie."

The next day, Joe went to the bank and withdrew fifty pounds. There was a time when they had just started courting and he'd used some of old Babba Matka's money to make a scandalously extravagant purchase. He'd bought Perl a small leather handbag on the black market. She had enthused emphatically, delighted that a man could choose something just the right size and such a great colour too; he was a genius, apparently.

Remembering this, on a whim he went into Woolworths on Erdington High Street and bought her a sequined purse with a tasselled zip. Before he went to work on the Thursday, he left the purse with the money on her bedside table with a note on the top. *Happy Anniversary.*

♦

"Phone, Boss!"

Josek flipped the sausages and, knocking down the temperature, jogged to the payphone in the café. It had taken an age to get it installed but Perl said it would get more people to come inside and she was right. They put a bright Buzby poster in the window to publicise the fact. *Make Someone Happy!* it proclaimed. It certainly made Perl happy. She was constantly ringing him on the bloody thing.

Lo and behold, it was Perl on the line; her voice sounded happy, light, bubbling with excitement. It was like he was listening to another woman.

"Thank you, darling. A beautiful gift! I would have come in to the shop but I've got to catch this bloody train..."

"It's okay. You enjoy yourself, sweetheart."

"Donna says I can stay until Sunday. Is that too long? She has – *what's it called?* – an 'itinerary' for me. We're going to see a band tonight and shopping tomorrow and she says I am not allowed to buy anything for the baby, and then we're going to a wine bar and if I am still standing after that she says the next day we will go to the Malvern Hills so I can see some proper English countryside."

"No, no, that's fine. Like I said, go mad!" But then he reconsidered. "Yeah but if you get tired, stop, okay? I don't want the baby born in a fucking wine bar."

◆

He could hear the happiness enveloping Perl; she was content and safe. Well, as safe as a woman could be in Donna's company. It afforded Josek permission to cease his worries, he thought, at least for a while.

He'd persuaded the younger of the two Daves to take over in the kitchen on the Friday and Saturday, and luxuriating in the novelty of solitude, decided he'd go up town and spend the evening at the Polish Millennium House. He and Perl had been a few times, although setting up the café had meant any kind of socialising was rare. Still, it was always pleasant to hear Polish voices and relax a little.

Maybe he'd have a drink. Dusk was falling as he stepped off the bus. Office workers filled the pavement of New Street and buttery lights from the shops shone on the lively traffic as he walked past the Odeon.

Now here was a thing.

He had just passed a pub – a small doorway – tucked between the shops. He remembered reading about this pub in the newspaper, and the bombs, before he and Perl had arrived, of course. So terrible. The pictures in the paper made it look like a wrecking ball had set to work. But see – it persisted, he thought.

He must have walked past this pub hundreds of times on Perl's endless errands, but he'd never had the opportunity to go inside.

The door was ajar. Curious, he turned, and went inside.

Going down the steps into the dark was comforting, like the bars in Gdansk, hot and smoky and with a line of barstools already occupied. City workers who'd clocked off for the day thronged the counter. He absorbed the banter and the drinking and the bubble of noise, that sweet smelling infusion of smoke and beer. The room was alive. Walking to the bar. he became part of the scene and he found it invigorating.

"You alright? Not seen you in here before."

The barmaid was brunette, wavy thick hair around a youthful, pretty face. She had the same open, friendly expression as his old friend Maria from the village, and the comparison, coupled with her manner, generated some sort of instantaneous trust.

"Josek. You can call me Joe. Well, you see, my wife is away..."

"So the cat will play?" She raised her thin eyebrows. "Only teasing, love." She smiled so sweetly at him as she said it that he relaxed a little.

He shuffled onto a bar stool and hunched warily, sharing a mischievous grin with this nice girl.

"Yes! I am 'playing' tonight."

The barmaid leaned on her side of the bar, mirroring him, arms crossed over her breasts looking intensely at him for a moment, part stern confessor, part conspirator.

"What are you playing at, Joe? You can tell me. I'm a brilliant listener."

"What's the word? Pleasing myself a little!" He wasn't sure if he'd got the phrasing quite right. He'd only know if there was vague confusion in the face of whoever he was talking to.

"Good for you."

"She's having our baby soon, you see, and I know babies keep you busy. I thought if I don't come and try an English beer in an English pub now, then I never will, right?"

She gave a wide grin, reached out and stroked his cheek like a loving mother.

"Just for that, Joe, your first English beer is on Tracey." She winked.

"Who the fuck's Tracey?" he asked, and then looked embarrassed as she pointed at herself, shaking her head and laughing. He was aware that someone had shuffled alongside him on the next barstool.

"Hey, you Polish?"

"Yeah, I am Polish."

"I'm Mike. Pleased to meet you, Polish." Mike crossed his hand awkwardly to shake Josek's.

"Well, my name is Josek, Mike."

Mike looked blankly at Josek. "Josie? No way mate, you're 'Polish' now."

Josek was about to correct him but Mike belched and it was clear that the conversation had moved on.

It was hard to say how old Mike was. He was shiny from his bald, red head to his pointy shoes. Heavy cufflinks winked at his sleeves. He reeked of what Josek believed to be *Paco Rabanne*. As much of a fan of a drop of cologne as the next man, Mike clearly was rather heavy-handed when applying the stuff.

He indicated a group of youths in checked shirts, with shaved heads and tattoos. Josek noticed they were eyeing him suspiciously. As he met their gaze they narrowed their eyes, and turned away, disguising their mutters behind white, bony fists.

Mike raised his chin at them with a sneer. "Don't worry about them, mate, they only really hate the Pakis."

Josek felt a thin strand of fear pull through his chest but really, these weasels were a joke. He wasn't, and had never been, much of a fighter, but even he could imagine giving them a slap if needed. They couldn't be much more than children. He must have grinned or smiled as Mike poked him and then tapped the bar.

"Yeah, but it's their dads you want to worry about."

"God damn, Mike, I wasn't worried about anything until I met you."

Mike scrutinised Josek's face and then laughed loudly, slapping Josek on the back.

♦

The Jukebox had been on a loop of *Maneater* by Hall & Oates for twenty minutes. Josek didn't feel like he'd been up since 4am, he felt wide awake and happy, accepting a cigarette from Mike, and then another, then another as the banter and the beer flowed.

"Joe's playing tonight – 'ent that right, Joe?" Tracey informed Mike.

"His name is Polish – I told you that already."

Josek shrugged and Tracey laughed, then reasoned, "Well that's a shit nickname if ever I heard one – can't you come up with anything better than that?"

"You want a better nickname? Okay." Mike belched again as he thought. "Alright, how about *shithead* or *wankarrr*," – this he articulated with a flourish of his hand, effecting a posh voice. "Either of those do you, Josie Joe?"

"I am okay with Polish." Josek had begun to giggle, unaccustomed to the lightness.

"So, playing away, eh?"

"I'm just having a beer. In the pub!"

"That's what *he* means by playing." Tracey pointed sympathetically at Josek.

"You're shitting me? Dear oh dear, Polish, me old mate. I'm going to have to give you an education."

"I don't need one mate, I'm happy. I got education enough."

"With the greatest of respect, Polish, if you think having a pint of the piss they serve here is 'playing' then you don't know the meaning of the word."

"I don't get out much – too busy setting up my business. Café. Up in Erdington."

"You poor bastard. Enjoy the view there, do you? Like spaghetti, do you?" Mike slapped Josek's thigh.

"We don't serve spaghetti. Full English."

He saw Mike and Tracey exchange a smirk, and then he received an indulgent smile which, whilst momentarily irritating, called to mind Maria's mother. Such indulgent smiles were often accompanied with a large plate of soup, or fried bread dipped in egg. He gulped his pint, thirsty at the recollection.

"Anyway, you'll never make any money out of food, mate."

"Everyone needs feeding. Food and family. That's all that matters."

"Beg to differ there, Polish. Talking of which... excuse me."

A tall, slim blonde had appeared at Mike's side, and she was wearing a stretchy, orange dress that ably demonstrated that she'd neglected to factor in underwear. Mike brought an arm around this doll and introduced her as Katie. The music and babble was so loud and fast that Josek couldn't keep up. He settled into his position on the stool, laughing at the way Mike was saying things, even though what he was saying was now unintelligible.

Katie had frothy blonde curls on top of her head in a pile and that bright makeup like Perl used to wear; he was reminded how lithe a body could be without the baby bump. He felt a shock of jealousy. Perl, he mulled, must be almost double the size she'd been when he met her. He hated her new haircut. He ruminated on all the things which had changed and been lost, and felt vaguely wistful

– for what exactly, he wasn't sure. Life was certainly better now. In any case, with the drink and the smoke and the music from the jukebox, not to mention Katie's dress, Josek found that his attention was focussed entirely on taking another large draught from his glass.

♦

It was a novelty to be walking home drunk, he thought, as he pottered in little zig-zags from the bus stop back to the house. He quite liked it. When he got home, instead of creeping and flinching at the creaks, he clicked on the lights and even turned the radio on.

Josek hiccupped, bobbing unsteadily as he levered off his shoes. He toppled onto the sofa and passed out.

♦

Once again, in his dreams he was back in the Poland of his childhood. With broad glorious days turning to generous pink twilights. This time, summer in the mountain, was his favourite time of all. He rarely dreamed of the snow.

Soft air – it buoyed his thin form like the warm water of the lagoon. So deep! Roman had dropped a rock from the parched pier – or was it a branch? – and they watched it fall out of sight. This gave them the courage to dive; Josek dart-like and fat Roman shrieking that he was the God of War as he landed heavily with a tremendously joyful splash. Gasping, rosy-faced and laughing, they were so happy.

Haze now. And then in Roman's mother's kitchen. She was the cleverest cook he knew; in fact, Josek thought she must be a witch to conjure such food out of the same potatoes and milk as everyone else. She wasn't an evil witch like Babba Matka, no, she was most definitely the good sort. She even had a spell book. She placed it on the table – opening it for him to see. It had a photograph inside of a table spread with the most delicious cakes and cold meats and puddings in tall glasses with purple and pink fruit on the top. The words *Ada Nowak's Modern Cookery* were bold in orange print on the hard cover.

Then Maria, bursting in, gabbling how she'd learned to cook something called French Toast from the instructions in this book of Ada Nowak's. Maria was so close to Roman in age, just a year or so older but as slim as her brother was solid; she was a lark, he was an owl. He smiled to see her, ruefully glancing at Roman; he wished Roman would allow his sister to join their games.

He liked Maria in particular because of this way that she talked and talked, her thoughts slipping in silky ribbons. Like now, she twittered and chattered about this wonderful thing she had learned to cook as if it was the most urgent news of the day. Again, a frequent remembrance, gaining colour and substance from his repeated imagining.

Maria related in detail the steps to turn dry bread into something crispy and delicious, so delicious you had to wipe your mouth the whole time you were eating it – or so she said. You dipped the bread into milk and then egg, and then dropped it into the hot skillet but for God's sake only for a moment else the milky insides go all dry and it's not the same, it's just not the same at all, she said. Her eyes were doleful at the tragedy of over-crisped toast. Josek felt a bubbling laugh at this thought, and she saw it, and she laughed at herself.

He said he would love to eat that; it sounded really nice. Maria said she would make it for Josek but not Roman. Roman had gone back to play anyway. Shrugging happily, she had run from the room.

Maria's mother again, watching him. She was as thin as a broom, which puzzled Josek. He supposed she must just give the children all the food and eat none herself. His mother used to do the same.

Then, back in the cottage, and he was asking his great-aunt, fat Babba Matka if she had any books with pictures of food in them, and despite being in good humour she cuffed him around the head and said recipe books were for sluts.

Then he was quiet. It never paid to provoke.

Slipping outside, the sun soaked into his small back, melding bruises into a generalised pleasant golden glow. Roman was there. He decided that they would make a sundial out of rocks using some kind of science he had learned in one of his father's books. Roman was looking for equal rocks. Josek was charged with drawing the most perfect circle he could in the largest dried-out flowerbed.

Stamping. He used his feet to stamp down the lumps. Stamping gave way to shuffling and he began to shuffle in a circle to pack down the earth. Round and round he went, spiralling out in a way that ensured the sundial would be round as the sun itself, Josek gained some sort of happy comfort from the rhythm of his shuffling feet. Left Right Left Right! He thought this might be how it felt to be a soldier or even a prisoner; this thought causing a sudden pause, which was convenient because Roman wanted to step across his path at the sight of a chunky flint. It would be a perfect number six because it matched the twelve, he said. He held them up to show Josek and he agreed. Two solid flints with the same seam.

Roman was so clever! Josek was not. He thought sometimes that his own mind must be shattered into a mass of tiny pieces inside, even though he looked like a normal boy.

Roman stopped in his flint searching to exclaim how smooth Josek's circle was, how perfectly round! Josek grinned with pride and he felt certain that at instants like this, here in the cracked mud-tracks or sometimes the meadows or the forest, how could these not be the happiest moments of his life? He wondered what could follow in life to match those instants and just ached at their brevity.

Maybe one whole day would be as happy, one day.

Sundown, the heat ebbing from their plans, although with childish momentum they urged the play on and on, fuelling the scheme for a few minutes more.

Here, out the back of Babba Matka's, they counted off one exact minute to see how long a minute was, crossing off the seconds in chalk on the side of the wall.

The sun finally tipped behind the trees and their beautiful sundial became almost invisible against the dry clods.

Josek's stomach clenched into a fist as the door opened. Babba Matka appeared in her strap-lashed aprons carrying a paper-covered parcel. "Slavbka. For your mother, Roman. Now go," she snapped, pushing the parcel of bread at Roman.

Josek could almost taste the plum-sour beer on her breath.

Warily eyeing Babba Matka, Roman jumped to his feet. "Thank you, Mrs Wrona."

"Call me Babba Matka."

He watched Babba Matka's simpering face. Whilst miserable he remembered his mother once more, and how she'd always said her aunt was an old witch. It was unfortunate for Josek that guardians were in thin supply for orphans.

Roman had disappeared from view. Babba Matka's simper became set in a line. Josek felt weak as his eyes saw hers surveying the chalk marks on the wall.

Josek knew what would come next. The fury, that was about to erupt, had needed permission, although almost anything would do when she was this soaked.

The Fury.

♦

He woke, groggy, with his hand awkwardly propped inside his underpants. He found that his arm was a dead weight, numb from crumpled sleep. It took some effort to retrieve his hand; he better check the time. Four AM. For a moment he was startled, nausea shocked into submission; then he recalled that Dave was covering and the nausea crept back, the better to lay claim on his sorry form.

He smelt disgusting. The smoke from the pub had wafted from his clothing, filling the room. A stale beer tang clung to the smell. It was no good, he had to get rid of this smell or he was going to vomit.

Josek stood slowly, stretching and wincing. Before he staggered to the shower, he undressed clumsily and placed the discarded clothes outside the back door. The sour smoky smells were giving rise to an anxious swell in his chest. He felt a little better as the cool night air blew in through the opened door before it shut, the tobacco-trapped clothes now firmly penned outside.

The water washed the scum away.

Family and food. Family and food. All that matters.

He remembered the drunk conversation with Mike, and Katie in her dress and then, ruefully, how he had felt angry about Perl.

He wondered once again what had become of Maria. Once Babba Matka had died, Josek had taken the old bitch's hoarded money to Gdansk and vowed never to go back. She'd been a terrible guardian but Maria and her family had at least showed him how things could be. Perl too. Fastidious and emotional as she undoubtedly could be, she was also kind and organised and able to say how she felt and she could return his love. She would be a wonderful mother. Yes. They were flints with the same seam.

Life was good. It had been one whole happy day. He felt certain that there would be others to come. Perhaps they would not be filled with sundials and lagoons, but he was not alone. There would be work and friendship, perhaps. Certainly, there was love. He was loved and could love. He persisted.

He thought about the baby, as he towelled himself off and put on clean jogging bottoms. He retrieved the clothes from the porch. He'd wash them. Then he'd hang them on the line to dry. The sun was coming up.

Nicky Tate lives in Smethwick with her sons, and works for a broadcast consultancy. She writes for radio, and also writes prose and screenplays for fun, and occasional profit. Mostly fun. Occasional fell-botherer. For more, see **nickytate.co.uk**

Philip's Decision: The English Civil War Comes to Birmingham

Miles Atkinson

Saturday 1ˢᵗ April, 1643, Aston Hall

The leaded windows of the library bathed the room in late afternoon sunshine.

"It matters not, boy," remarked Sir Thomas. "Such hearty and wilful disaffection towards His Majesty will not go unpunished. I respect your wish to remain uncommitted in the present troubles, Philip, but that is a luxury you can no longer afford – especially if you wish to wed Lucinda."

Sir Thomas sipped his wine, nodded appreciatively and glared at the young man opposite him.

"Thank you, Crawford, you may go."

The steward bowed and stepped back.

"Not the wine. That can stay!"

With another bow, the man retreated and the door of the library clicked shut behind him.

Philip Daubney stared helplessly at the floor. His six-month acquaintance with Lucinda Lambton had developed in a manner and at a speed neither of them had been expecting. Matters had *culminated* the previous afternoon as the pair of them had walked, disgracefully unchaperoned, in Aston Park.

"*There is no sin in eschewing the madness of this conflict, Philip. If you can do that in Birmingham, then surely I can do no less here at Aston Hall.*"

Her clear grey eyes sought his as she gently stroked his cheek.

"I love you, Philip – no woman gives herself to a man as I have done unless she desires nothing more than to be his wife. Sir Thomas will not refuse you if you seek his permission now."

Sir Thomas was speaking again. "You've given good service these past six months – no mean feat for a lawyer in a town rife with unrepentant Puritan rebels. Alas, events are moving in the war and the time has come for you to declare for one side – or the other."

He looked expectantly at Philip, who tried to appear attentive. Sir Thomas Holte, Justice of the Peace for His Majesty King Charles, was not fooled.

"Wits wool-gathering again, boy, or were you reviewing the charms of my ward?"

Philip blushed helplessly as the old man brought up the real reason for his visit to Aston Hall. Bright blue eyes twinkled with amusement at his discomfort.

"In truth," continued Sir Thomas, "it is mostly about Lucinda that I wished to speak to you. Were she my daughter I would price her so high that no upstart lawyer, however well-connected, could afford her. She is not, though, and before her father died I promised him I would secure his daughter a suitable match."

Philip opened his mouth to speak but the old knight cut him off abruptly.

"Have the grace to hear me out, boy. You seem to have stolen her heart these three months gone; the girl has eyes for none but you. Your father and brother may well have sided with the Rebels but God knows yours is not the only family in England thus divided. You are young, with gentry connections and, God-willing, good prospects. There is but one condition before I give my permission to the marriage."

"That being that I publicly renounce the Parliament, I assume?" Philip cursed inwardly – he hated the old man for his smug, knowing manner and easy assumption of obedience. He realised that he'd spoken more coldly than he'd intended, something borne out by the flash of anger in the old man's eyes.

"I suggest you moderate your tone, Master Daubney, but in essence yes, that is what I require."

He took a sip of wine and regarded Philip in silence. Finally, he spoke again, his voice precise and cold - as if he were delivering judgement at the local assizes. "You will return to Birmingham immediately. You have until noon on Tuesday to put your business affairs in order. By sunset on that day you will have taken up residence at Aston Hall. Birmingham is an unfit residence for my ward's betrothed."

Philip's emotions must have shown in his face, for Sir Thomas sighed and appeared to relent. "Forgive me. I spoke more harshly than you deserve. Please, sit down."

Reluctantly, Philip moved to sit opposite him and the old man refilled his own glass and poured another, which he pushed towards Philip.

Sir Thomas finally broke the silence. "Think of me what you will. Lucinda is my responsibility and one I take seriously. With the country in civil war, that includes ensuring she's married both well and safely. You understand my position I'm sure."

Philip sighed and nodded.

The old man raised his wine glass and leaned forward.

"Once you are here, not only would you and Lucinda be together but you would also be under my protection. No, hear me out, boy. The war turns in His Majesty's favour - especially in the Midlands. Brereton was turned back at Hopton Heath not two weeks ago and Lichfield cannot hope to hold out for much longer. Remember too that I am not without influence at Court. Intercession on behalf of your father and brother would be a much easier course of action with you already at my side."

"So, all my heart's desire will cost me is... my self-respect."

With highly-placed protection for your family when Parliament finally comes to terms with the King.

Sir Thomas snorted derisively. "Such naivety ill becomes a lawyer. I am offering you the best chance to match your desires to your circumstances and thereby protect your family. Are you really such a fool as to reject it?"

There was a sudden outburst of noise outside the door. Crawford's voice could be heard raised in protest, then the door opened and a uniformed figure strode into the room and swept Sir Thomas a bow.

"Lieutenant Rupert Ingles sir, Sir John Byron's Regiment of Horse. I have an urgent message for you ..." He paused, taking in Philip. "A *private* message, sir."

"Then hand it over", said the old man briskly. Ingles pulled a letter from his buff coat.

Sir Thomas took it, broke the seal and read the contents. His eyes widened noticeably, a reaction swiftly brought under control. He looked up sharply at the Royalist officer, who was glancing curiously at Philip.

Adjusting the red sash around his waist, Ingles shuffled uncomfortably. "I must return to my regiment but before I go I have some word-of-mouth."

"Naturally," Sir Thomas purred. "If you would be so good as to wait in the parlour, Crawford will see to your needs and I will join you shortly."

Lieutenant Ingles bowed deeply, replaced his hat and exited the room.

Philip opened his mouth to speak, but Sir Thomas ignored him.

"Some matters have arisen that require my immediate attention. I should like you to leave now and think well upon what we have discussed." He broke off, staring thoughtfully through the leaded windows. "Whatever you decide to do, Philip, please don't take too long." He rose, indicating that the conversation was at an end.

Philip recalled the way the letter had been read and quickly secured. Something had been written there which had both surprised and worried the old man. Sir Thomas placed one hand on Philip's shoulder and, for a moment, his expression almost seemed one of pity. Then his face hardened, and, he escorted him out into the entrance hall.

Philip felt rather like an unwanted client of his father's. What would have prompted the old man to end their discussion so quickly?

Philip's horse was saddled and awaiting him outside. Clearly, he was being invited to leave at his earliest convenience.

Sir Thomas gave him a brisk nod. "A safe journey, Philip, and for the sake of my ward may God give you the grace to make the right decision."

For a couple of seconds, he appeared about to say more, but seemed to recollect himself and instead lifted a hand in farewell.

With nothing more to say, Philip returned the gesture and steered his horse away.

♦

The bridge across the deer trap at the edge of Aston Park vibrated briefly under the hooves of Philip's horse. The road crested a short rise and then the valley of the river Rea spread before him. The sun was beginning to set and the warmth of the day still lingered on the pastures and rough grazing land that sloped away towards the river as it hurried on its way to join the Tame.

The view would normally have filled Philip with quiet contentment, but his mind was in such turmoil that he scarcely noticed it.

Father will understand, won't he? Oh, most assuredly. The agreement was that you'd have six months to see if remaining neutral was going to be an option in this war. Not to fall in love with the ward of the area's most prominent Royalist! Oh Father, what am I to do?

His mother would have counselled him to follow his heart, but Lady Clara Daubney was dead these fifteen summers past, her still-born daughter with her. Sir John Daubney had thrown himself into his work as legal advisor to Sir Edward Nicholas, the Secretary of State. Tried, in the best traditions of the Daubney family, to counsel both Sir Edward and the King but to no avail. So, over six months ago, Major Sir John Daubney had raised a troop of horse and taken them to join the Earl of Essex's army. Philip's only surviving sibling Adam had gone with him, the ink still wet on his cornet's commission.

They had to go. Father was adamant about that. Equally determined that one of his sons should survive the horrors of a civil war. You saw it didn't you Father? The plague-ridden streets of Nuremberg and the ashes of Magdeburg? That such things might be visited upon Englishmen by other Englishmen was an abomination.

Philip looked up.

His horse, patient and sensible old Blossom, knew the way home better than he did and had already found the Stafford road and he coaxed her into a steady trot as the spire of St Martin's church appeared out of the twilight haze. The smoke from the blade mills along the river still lingered in the air as Blossom cut along a track that brought them out into New Hall Lane. Lights twinkled gently in the distant windows of New Hall as they passed the top of Pinfold Lane and the first buildings of the town proper. At the very top of New Street stood three large half-timbered houses, built in the newest style. A stone arch linked the first two and Philip rode through it into a compact stable yard.

He was home.

The Daubney townhouse, New Street, Birmingham

"Will you be wanting supper, Master Philip?"

Apart from the single lamp burning in the parlour, the Daubney townhouse was in darkness.

Jane Rogers was one of the two servants his father had kept on and one of the most efficient and unflappable. Yet the normally imperturbable Jane appeared flustered and, on closer inspection, nearer to outright fear than Philip had ever seen her.

"In God's name, Jane, what on earth is happening?" Jane brushed a strand of loose grey hair back under her cap as Philip removed his coat and flung it across the settle.

"Oh sir, people are saying that the Malignants are coming to punish us for last autumn. The Coventry men have returned to Lichfield, so how shall Birmingham stand against the enemy?"

She fell silent, hands working helplessly at her apron.

Philip spoke slowly, doing his best to project calmness and confidence. "Sit down, Jane, take a deep breath and recover yourself. Now, tell me exactly where you heard this talk."

The maid regained her composure, just as her brother Samuel entered with a tray of bread, cheese and ale.

"Blossom's rubbed down and fed, sir." Looking around he spied his sister and his face set in a frown.

"I do hope Jane hasn't been worrying you with the latest gossip, Master Philip. There've been lots of contrary rumours flying today."

Philip helped himself to the bread and cheese and gestured to Samuel to sit down too.

"Actually, she hasn't had the opportunity to tell me anything of substance yet, gossip or otherwise." Gesturing to Jane to continue, he filled three mugs with ale from the jug and pushed two of them across the table. Taking a cautious sip from one of them the servant continued.

"Well, sir, it was midday when word came that news had arrived from Henley. Seemingly, some of the drovers working between Birmingham and Henley are saying that Prince Rupert is coming north from Oxford..."

"With an army?" The words had barely left his mouth before Philip cursed himself for their idiocy.

No, you lack wit, he fancies taking that poodle of his for a walk in the Warwickshire countryside. Of course he's bringing a bloody army!

Tactfully affecting not to have heard, Samuel sipped his own ale.

"If his uncle's sent him anywhere, sir, it's like to be Lichfield." Taking a sip of his own, Philip reflected on that for a moment.

"Your brother has the right of it, I think, Jane. The Queen is in Yorkshire with much needed powder and ball. The King must secure Lichfield if she's to safely move south. We are too small a fish here."

Jane smiled nervously, "I pray so, sir, for the town is not defensible."

"That being to our advantage," remarked Philip, "for if the Malignants do come, we shall give them no cause to attack us."

"Like as not," commented Samuel as he stood and drained his mug. Philip followed suit and all three readied themselves for sleep.

"Best not borrow trouble, in the clear light of day this is like to be nothing but rumours."

Sunday 2nd April, St Martin's Church

The late morning sun lanced down through the chancel windows. Mr. Roberts, Philip reflected, definitely preached a fine sermon.

"My brothers and sisters, we must not give way to fear. The Lord is our salvation and in him alone must we trust. It is the King's arrogance and the evil of his advisers that have brought the country to this pass. As Scripture says, there shall be wars and rumours of wars but these things are but the birth pains."

Philip smiled to himself.

The Minister was an inspiring figure, his voice both at once authoritative and reassuring. Unbidden, the face of Lucinda came before his mind's eye and abruptly, his mood changed. Yet again, he shied away from a decision the magnitude of which he was only now beginning to realise. Would his father and brother understand if he put love before family?

"Philip, I respect your right to decide for yourself which course to follow and your wish to remain publicly uncommitted. New Hall needs a master and your idea to set up in practice in Birmingham needs to be explored. Remember though, in a war such as this you may not have the luxury of indecision for long. You have a year to decide. If the war has not ended by next October, you must make your choice."

A sudden hubbub from the back of the church. There was a chorus of indistinct shouting and then the main door flew back on its hinges with a loud boom. A tattered, travel-stained figure staggered up the nave, looking about him wildly. One half of his face was a mask of dried blood, the other covered by an equally bloodstained bandage. A man in his late 30s, he would have been well-dressed, if his clothing had not been ripped and liberally spattered with mud. Obviously in the last stages of exhaustion, he gazed around the church wildly. Finally, his gaze lighted upon Mr. Roberts. Staggering to the foot of the pulpit, he appeared to reach up one hand as if in supplication.

"Prince Rupert," he gasped, "two thousand horse and foot and four field pieces. Coming to punish us all. God have mercy..." His eyes rolled up and he collapsed, just as the church exploded into panicked uproar.

Two hours later, Birmingham Guildhall

As public meetings went, thought Philip wearily, this was achieving nothing.

"Will he live?" Mr. Roberts lent back in his chair in the meeting room of the Guildhall.

Mr. Cunliffe the surgeon nodded cautiously.

"With God's grace, yes. Head wounds are problematic, but the skull is not fractured and he shows no sign of the mental confusion often present after such injury."

The presence of the leading worthies of Birmingham was, Philip thought, made worse by the presence of those who aspired to that role. The room was a babble of several simultaneous arguments that was only brought to order when one of the army officers present bellowed for silence. Philip recognised Captain Greaves, commander of Birmingham's sole troop of horse.

The babble of voices stilled.

Greaves turned to Mr. Roberts, who continued.

"Thank you, gentlemen," said Philip. "I realise we're all gravely concerned by our visitor's news and what it portends. For that very reason we must make clear decisions unencumbered by pride and self-delusion."

He was not entirely sure why he had been included in this meeting, but it seemed that the standing in which his father had been held had transferred itself, at least in part, to him. He took a deep breath and ventured a question.

"Who is he?"

Captain Greaves pursed his lips thoughtfully. "His name's Enderby - he's a tailor from Stratford who picked a bad time to be visiting relatives in Henley. Seems as if the poor bastard ran straight into Rupert's picquet just outside the town. Thinking him one of our spies, they roughed him up and were going to do for him properly when *meinherr* Rupert decided he was more use as a calling card and sent him on his way here."

The outcry from the various town worthies within earshot was only drowned out by Mr. Roberts hammering the heel of one hand on the table before him.

"In God's name, gentlemen," he bellowed, "we will have order here". As the minister glared around the room, silence gradually returned. "Thank you. Now then, Captain Greaves and I say the town is indefensible, yet despite this you say some show of force must be made. We would hear your reasons."

The three men who stood were well known to Philip. Even in Birmingham, all three were notable for their antipathy towards the King and any who supported him. Richard Hunt was a well-to-do cobbler and his two sidekicks, Sam Ellesmore and William Ward were equally well-known in the blade making industry in the town. Ward and Hunt looked determinedly at Ellesmore, who came to stand alongside them.

"Sir, if the Malignants are coming, it is with the intent to sack and despoil the town. Why else would they come in such numbers, if not to have their revenge for last autumn?"

Ward was also a good speaker, Philip thought, simple and direct and disinclined to be overly emotional – unlike the other two.

"More like," chimed in Ellesmore, "they mean to settle accounts with us first and then move on Lichfield."

Ward nodded in agreement as others from the audience called out in Ellesmore's support.

Captain Greaves shook his head sadly.

"Gentlemen, one bank and ditch will not stop a determined assault. One company of foot and one troop of horse are simply insufficient."

Minister Roberts raised his right hand in a futile attempt to stop the chorus of angry denial from the rest of those present.

"This is not Thermopylae, and while I respect your gallantry, I have no wish to see you emulate Leonidas' Spartans."

"The Minister is right - four field pieces, seven hundred foot and a thousand horse mean you would be going to your deaths. Even if Rupert comes against us directly, we can hold the Kempe's Hill earthwork for no more than an hour or two."

"Then we shall barricade the crossings over the Rea and arm the townsfolk."

Greaves looked incredulously at him.

"Are you quite mad, sir? Have you any conception of what the laws and usages of war prescribe for civilians taken in arms?"

Captain Greaves was quite unprepared for the tirade of invective that followed.

The Daubney townhouse, New Street

The late spring afternoon was darkening. Philip took a deep gulp of wine as a coldly dispassionate part of his mind regarded his trembling right-hand and despised his obvious weakness. Surely, his father would understand. Lucinda had given herself to him freely and willingly, an action which required a clear and obvious response. Except that in this case, it was very far from obvious. All he had to do was to be back at Lucinda's side – at the side of the woman who loved him, by tomorrow morning. Her honour would be intact and so would...

My honour?

He looked up at the row of portraits. Sir Miles Daubney, Master of the Horse to the old queen, regarded him with cynical amusement. Ralph Daubney, gentleman of the bedchamber to King Henry VIII stared back with cold contempt.

He walked to the final picture and looked up. Of course, as his father had often said, this was really the first picture – the man who had brought the Daubney name out of obscurity and into the ranks of the gentry.

The picture never failed to give Philip gooseflesh - largely because he might so easily have been looking at himself. The slight, blonde haired man sitting in the high-backed chair wore the doublet and hose in fashion nearly 200 years previously. The woman standing behind him (in total defiance of convention) wore the gown and kirtle of the same period. The man's clothing was of good but not extravagant quality, as was the woman's.

Philip had always wondered at this picture – the man (possibly a few years older than himself) was looking out of the picture, an expression of peace and tranquillity on his face.

The woman, by contrast, was gazing straight down at him from her position behind his chair. Long, slender hands rested protectively on his shoulders, maybe even possessively. Her jet-black hair was mostly covered by a tight headdress and her slender face had an austere beauty.

"Looking for inspiration from Sir Gervaise and Lady Philippa, sir?"

Philip jumped in shock and a large quantity of wine splashed onto the floor.

"For the love of God, Samuel, don't sneak up on me like that." Suddenly weak with relief, Philip collapsed into a nearby chair.

The servant swiftly sized up his employer's demeanour and expression, opening his mouth to make a fulsome apology. Then, he saw the fear in Philip's eyes and nodded grimly.

"I know, Sir; they're going to make a fight of it. That's why I took the liberty of sending Jane to my brothers in Edgbaston – with God's mercy, she'll be safe enough there. I hope..."

Here, he broke off and stared at the floor.

"No, Samuel, you did entirely the right thing. In fact, before this night is much older I want you to join her. Take my horse, if the worst happens, I know where to find you."

So that my betrayal of family, name and honour will have no immediate witnesses except God himself.

Samuel had almost refused point-blank, as Philip had known he would. As he watched horse and rider disappear into the darkness at the top of New Street, Philip realised that only one bridge remained to be burned. As he returned to the library and the alcoholic solace it contained, he could not have said which disturbed him the more, the anticipation of seeing Lucinda again or the feelings of self-contempt that threatened to make any attempt to sleep a futile one.

Monday 3rd April

The distant boom that woke him wrenched his head from the library table. A shaft of morning sunlight made him squint, curse and bitterly regret the previous night's overindulgence. Another boom, less deep this time, but still enough to make the window vibrate.

Philip staggered to his feet, clutching at the table. His head pounded and the sour taste in his mouth made him want to vomit.

And so you hit a new low, don't you, boy? As if drowning your problems in what is left of father's wine would wash them away. Idiocy...

What in the name of all that's holy was that noise?

As another series of dull booms made the windowpanes tremble, Philip realised that for the first time in his life he was hearing cannon fire.

A hurried visit to the pump, some hastily applied cold water (his stomach revolted at the thought of food), and he was fumbling on hat and coat. He emerged into a practically deserted New Street and hurried down it past the Guildhall. As he entered Manor Place, more dull thuds shook the air.

The market stalls and shops surrounding St Martin's church and the Corn Cheaping bullring appeared locked and shuttered, the few people he encountered intent on closing and in some cases barricading their homes.

"Ah, Master Daubney, whither away on this fine morning of the Lord's wrath?"

Even for a lunatic, Mr. Whitehall certainly had poise and presence. Taller than Mr Roberts, with broad shoulders and thickly curled dark hair, he cut a commanding figure. Newcomers to Birmingham often mistook him for the Minister. Still in his Sunday best, he held his prayer book before him like a shield and eyed Philip gravely.

"Are you familiar with the term Nemesis, boy?" Before Philip could reply or begin to extricate himself he continued, raising one arm and declaiming loudly.

"A righteous infliction of retribution manifested by an appropriate agent, that's what. Can you think of one more appropriate to deliver us our just desserts than the Prince of Malignants himself?"

The distant cannon boomed again, followed by cries of panic from the houses around them.

"Mr. Whitehall, sir, you must seek shelter, the church perhaps...?"

Whitehall's voice rose to a near scream.

"It is Nemesis I tell you, God's bloodied destruction sent upon us for our rebellious presumption, for our arrogance." He paused and grabbed Phillip's shoulders. "May the Lord send you a fair deliverance, only in God's name choose well," his voice faded to a near whisper, "as we all must this day."

Philip felt as if iced water had flowed down his neck, for the words were the right ones for what was in his mind.

And what kind of choice is it that will wound forever one of the two people dearest to you? If you start walking now, you could be at Aston Hall in hours.

Or, you can simply follow the sound of the guns and let them dull your senses to the truth that this choice is only yours to make.

Whitehall's voice positively vibrated with mad glee. "Seek expiation in blood, then boy, run to damnation with the rest of us."

His voice softened suddenly and his expression cleared, "Don't be afraid, Philip, God never gives us more than we can bear. Trust in Him, and you will know what to do."

With a final squeeze of the shoulder, he turned away and was lost to view between two nearby buildings.

◆

A short while later, he had reached the outbuildings of Mr. Porter's blade mill and could see that the two bridges over the river Rea had been barricaded. A score of townspeople crouched there, clutching a motley collection of swords, billhooks, a few pistols and the occasional musket. They looked frightened but resolute – some, recognising him, shouted his name as he ran past but he ignored them, wriggling between two overturned carts and emerging finally into Deritend. He ran on, driven by a wild reckless curiosity, seeking refuge from the burden of choice in the only way now open to him. As he rounded the final corner, the last buildings gave out and he came to a sudden halt.

He had found the battle.

Ahead of him, a belt of woodland partially obscured the scattered cottages of Bordsley. Figures moved just inside the wood line, their number and purpose obscured by a haze of grey-white powder smoke. The ditch and bank blocked the end of the Deritend Road and behind it crouched a double line of men. They hurriedly loaded their muskets, placed them ready on the aiming rods and poured powder into the pan.

As Philip crouched in the shadow of the last cottage, a steady roll of drums rang out across the field. The hedge of pikes that resolved itself from the powder smoke came on at a measured pace, four ranks of musketeers supporting it on either flank. Philip felt his guts churn horribly as the blue-coated Royalist foot pushed forward.

The gentle cough behind him made his heart lurch in sudden panic as he spun around.

"Terrible as an army with banners..." Mr. Roberts's voice was curiously flat and devoid of expression. In fact, thought Philip, he appeared close to despair.

Mr Roberts essayed a thin smile. "You'll recall my counsel of last night, Philip, how I pleaded that we show no resistance. As you see, I was overruled."

"So, are we to resist to the last? And, since we have shown fight, will the laws and usages of war protect us when we surrender?"

"The likes of Ward and Hunt demanded some show of resistance. Captain Greaves and Captain Girdler would be shamed; they and their men open even to charges of cowardice..."

"Then at what point will they regard their honour satisfied? If..."

The crash of muskets discharging in a rippling volley blotted out further comment.

All along the attacking line, men appeared to stumble, to be snatched backwards or simply to fall to both knees.

A second volley from the defenders stopped them in their tracks and, to the accompaniment of jeers from the defenders, they began to withdraw.

"Thus God defends the right!" Mr. Roberts' black mood had evaporated and, as Prince Rupert's blue coats retreated, he became almost jubilant.

Philip looked down at the equally enthusiastic defenders.

The few townspeople among them waved their borrowed muskets in the air and yelled abuse across the field. The sight disturbed Philip; he knew from accounts of the fighting in the Low Countries that civilians taken in arms faced severe reprisals. Yet this was England and surely even in a Civil War...

The tree line along the edge of Bordsley suddenly produced four great gouts of smoke. An instant later, three eruptions of earth exploded from the front of the bank and a wide ragged hole was smashed in the front of the cottage next to them.

Mr. Roberts' attempt to drag Philip to the floor was unnecessary – his legs had already given way.

◆

Two hours later, the ditch and banks still held. A few of Girdler's musketeers sported bloodstained bandages and the field leading up to the ditch was speckled with blue coated bodies. Some still moved, with the horrible slowness of crushed beetles.

The two onlookers had retreated to a drainage ditch alongside the road.

Mr. Roberts grinned with pride as he surveyed the defenders. "God's blood, Philip, but I hadn't looked for such resolve."

Philip found to his surprise that the bowel loosening fear had faded. Two infantry attacks and over an hour of bombardment and they were still alive. For how much longer though?

From the royalist lines came a sudden high, clear trumpet call. As it was repeated, line after line of mounted men appeared from the tree line. Sunlight gleamed dully from their breast plates as they drew up.

Laughter from behind the ditch and bank, a few insults and catcalls.

Philip looked on, appalled. Their defences would be as impassable to horse as to foot, if not more so.

The Minister did not seem so sure. Clambering from the ditch, he began to run down to the defenders, calling out for Captain Girdler.

What in God's name was he up to?

Then, Philip's gaze moved to the open fields on either side of their position and at last he understood. So too did Prince Rupert it seemed. A blade of trumpets announced the approach of the Royalist horse. As they cantered down the field they split into two wings. Each swept around the defenders' position well beyond musket shot, to the unguarded ford across the river, the open back gardens and tiny fences of Deritend and there was nothing and no one to stop them.

◆

A flying splinter of wood sliced across Phillips' cheek and he swore, cowering behind the overturned carts blocking Digbeth Road. His heart hammered from the lung bursting run up Deritend and his hair was matted with sweat and dust.

Mr. Roberts crouched beside him with Captain Girdler.

"For the love of God, Captain, is honour not now satisfied, or must the bloodshed continue?"

"If you think we can end it as easily as that then you're a naive fool, Minister."

A ragged volley from the defenders of the barricade was rewarded with several screams of agony and, as the choking powder smoke cleared, three bodies lay sprawled on the street. Three others were being dragged away by their comrades – one of these suddenly spun round, blood fountaining from his head to lie sprawled on the cobbles with the rest. Girdler swore vilely – the shot had come from one of the houses, a fact not lost on the royalist soldiers.

While the foremost men formed a firing line across the road, several others broke down the door of the nearest house and disappeared inside.

A chorus of the most terrible shrieks Philip had ever heard was followed by a single pistol shot.

A soldier (an officer by his red sash) emerged dragging behind him a boy of no more than fourteen. He spoke curtly to one of his men who produced a white cloth and began to wave it repeatedly over his head.

"I was expecting this," muttered Girdler, "will you join me, Minister?"

Shakily, Mr. Roberts rose and, despite his fear Philip did so as well.

"Lower your muskets damn you," he called to his men, "this is a flag of truce and the first man to ignore it pays with his life."

Looking across the barricade, Philip could see the royalist officer, a slender man whose flowing hair was badly singed. He handed the trembling boy over to another soldier, before approaching the barricade.

"Is there anyone in this rabble with the authority to speak?"

Despite his fear, Philip felt a flash of irritation. A gentleman (whether real or self-proclaimed) had a responsibility to try to act as one and it seemed as if this coolly aristocratic man was attempting to provoke a reaction.

There were growls of anger from behind the barricade and more than one man's hand strayed towards sword hilt. A furious glare from their captain ended any further movement.

Minister Roberts began to speak but Girdler placed one hand on his arm and addressed the royalist officer. His eyes took in the man's haughty bearing and he took a step forward.

The royalist recoiled, looking alarmed, "I am a messenger under a flag of truce and may not be assailed."

"Where such laws hold, it is also customary for a messenger to be less insolent." Girdler smiled thinly. "Might I have your name?"

"Major Lucius Hampton of His Highness Prince Rupert's Regiment of Foot. I have a message for the commander of the garrison, such as it is." Hampton had been fighting to keep his expression neutral, but could not resist a sneer with that last sentence.

"I would say that it has been a somewhat larger bite to swallow than you anticipated... Sir."

Hampton's jaw muscles clenched, but he otherwise made no response.

Girdler continued, "I might be prepared to surrender, given free passage for myself and my men."

Hampton and the soldiers with him exchanged glances.

"As a soldier, I applaud your gallant defence captain, but matters have arisen that make such an easy resolution impossible." He gestured to the soldier holding the boy and the man flung the lad roughly forward, causing him to fall to the cobbles at Hampton's feet, where he lay crying.

"The protection you speak of does not extend to civilians who choose to take up arms, and the laws and usages of war specify a clear punishment."

Without warning, his sword swept from its scabbard, straightened and plunged straight between the boy's shoulder blades. The impact forced the air from his lungs, as his mouth opened wide in an anguished scream. Hampton gave the sword of vicious twist, and ripped it free. A gout of blood burst from the boy's mouth as he lay face down, he spasmed twice and was still.

Philip felt bile rise in his mouth. He had heard of such things happening abroad, but here in England?

Hampton wiped his sword clean on the boy's jacket but did not resheath it, keeping it held out to one side.

"What you have just seen will be the fate of any civilian in this town who attacks one of my men and I can assure you that neither age nor sex will be accepted as a defence."

Cries of anger and grief rose from behind the barricade.

Girdler had opened his mouth, possibly to shout an order to his men, when a clatter of hoof beats made him spin round. One of Captain Greaves's troopers had brought his horse to a slewing halt just behind the defenders.

"In the name of Christ get your men back Sir," he screamed, "the Malignants are at Porter's blade mill."

Within seconds, there was a swirl of savage action. Several Royalist muskets discharged in quick succession. One shot hit the man in front of Philip; the impact of the ball opened his throat. With the dying man's blood speckling his face, Philip took to his heels, Mr Roberts behind him.

♦

Philip could never afterwards remember the full details of how he, with Mr. Roberts in tow, managed to reach Manor Place. Pure instinct guided him through the narrow alleys that ran parallel to Digbeth High Street, dodging and weaving through back gardens and, in one case, straight through someone's house and out the other side.

Behind them, the noise of musket fire lessened somewhat, but both men were horrified to see plumes of smoke marking the progress of Prince Rupert's men up the street towards the Guildhall.

Girdler and his men were nowhere to be seen – all that remained was the distant crackle of flames and the furious shouting of the royalist troops.

"May God have mercy on us," muttered Mr. Roberts, "for Prince Rupert will surely have none."

Philip's mind was so shaken that words failed him. After a while, he got to his feet and led the Minister on past the Guildhall to the junction with New Street.

"Sir, we must get off the street and look to our protection I..." Philip broke off, staring helplessly at the cobbles, quite shocked to find that he was weeping.

"So much blood,", he whispered "from so small a body." A fit of trembling took him and he lent against the wall. He felt Mr. Roberts's hand on his shoulder.

"There is little that I can say that will comfort you, Philip, this is war..."

"This is murder, sir, plain and simple and those who commit such crimes are not fit to...." The troop of horse that burst out of the New Street junction wiped any further comment from his mind. Only the direction from which they had come and their obvious orange sashes prevented panicked flight.

Their leader raised a hand to hold his men and drew his horse level with Philip.

Captain Greaves looked down at him, his expression a mixture of anguish and fury. "For the love of God, Daubney, get yourself and the Minister behind a barred door and stay there until you hear otherwise from me. I'm placing Mr. Roberts in your charge - the Malignants will want him and I would rather not have his blood on my conscience."

Philip opened his mouth to speak, but Captain Greaves interrupted him ruthlessly, "In God's name man, away!" Turning to the young officer next to him he gave a brisk nod. The man blew a high, ringing note on his cornet at which the entire mass of horsemen moved off at a brisk trot towards Corn Cheaping.

Recovering himself, Philip led the way up New Street and after a few minutes had barred the door of his house behind them.

Entering the parlour, both sank down at the table, weak with relief and exhaustion. After a while, Philip looked up.

"My apologies, Mr. Roberts, I'm not a very good host."

The Minister smiled ruefully, "Apologies unnecessary, just now I'm probably not the best of guests."

The pantry still had some bread and cheese and Philip commandeered this, together with two glasses and the remaining bottle of wine. Roberts politely declined the wine, but accepted a small cup of ale. When they'd both eaten, Philip got to his feet and checked cautiously outside.

Only to leap back into the doorway as Greaves' troop came past the house at a headlong gallop, Prince Rupert's cavalry just behind them.

◆

Twilight found both men still huddling in the parlour. They lit no fire and spoke only in whispers. Since the flight of Greaves' men, they had heard no further sounds of fighting, but several new plumes of smoke rose into the evening air from the centre of the town and confused shouting and screaming carried to them on the breeze.

Philip found himself trembling violently. At first he feared it was his former terror returning but this was different – although what exactly? After some time, he realised it was anger. Not a berserk unthinking rage but a cold fury at what was being done to his town.

And will Sir Thomas share your feelings do you think? Will Lucinda?

That was a train of thought he did not want to pursue but, as Birmingham suffered around him, he realised that he had no alternative left but to face the obvious answer. He rose abruptly and went to the bureau in the corner of the room. Returning with pen, paper and ink he sat down and tried to order his thoughts but without success. No words could justify what he was about to do, no action of his could expiate one of the worst forms of betrayal.

His mind whirled in a fresh burst of indecision.

If you aren't prepared to give up everything for love, then perhaps it was never love to begin with but something – baser. No, that's not true!

Isn't it? If you loved Lucinda as you profess to then you would already be by her side. The fact that you're skulking here is all the proof you need of your true feelings, if not your rank cowardice.

He suddenly realised that Mr. Roberts had been speaking for some time.

"I must get to Stafford, Philip – my life is probably forfeit here. Will you ride with me and see me safe to my brother's house?"

As the words of agreement passed his lips, Philip felt the burden of indecision that had plagued him for weeks begin to lift. There was no corresponding lightness of heart though.

In the stable yard he swiftly saddled his remaining horse and then filled the saddlebags with the last food in the house. Both he and Mr. Roberts kept to the side streets as they led their mount towards the Stafford Road. Three royalist troopers were busy ransacking the houses near the Guildhall, all foully drunk. They moved hurriedly into a side street, Philip keeping a firm hand on the horse's bridle. Cautiously they peered out.

Three bodies, all civilian, lay crumpled in the road and, somewhere close at hand, a woman shrieked. The soldiers approached one of the bodies and dragged it roughly upright. At that point the bonfire they'd made of smashed furniture flared up and the man they held between them was caught in its light. Both Philip and Mr Roberts barely stifled cries of surprise.

Mr Whitehall had clearly been badly beaten. One eye was swollen shut and there was blood on his face. His clothes were muddied and torn and the two soldiers who pinned his arms behind his back had to hold him upright.

"Alright, Roberts, you ranting Puritan bastard, this is your last chance. Swear loyalty to His Majesty the King and we won't cut your throat."

Hidden in the shadows of the side street, the two onlookers exchanged incredulous glances.

With a great effort, Mr Whitehall drew himself up to his full height.

"I will be damned sir, before I swear loyalty to such a perjured Papist King." Whereupon he spat full in the speaker's face. All three soldiers froze for an instant, before exploding into savage action. Thrusting Whitehall away from them, they drew their swords and, without a word, hacked him down. All three stabbed and slashed at the twitching body until it lay still.

♦

Wiping their blades clean on Whitehall's doublet, his killers sheathed their blades and disappeared into the alleyways alongside the Guildhall. Appalled and sickened, the two witnesses cautiously emerged into the street.

The hacked and twisted mass of flesh that had once been Mr. Whitehall lay in a spreading pool of blood. His Bible had been trampled into the dirt beside him. Philip wiped vomit from his mouth and struggled to put his thoughts into words.

Minister Roberts knelt by the body, head bowed, hands clasped his lips moving soundlessly. After a while he looked up at Philip, face anguished.

"May God have mercy on his soul. Poor, poor man – that should have been me lying there."

But it isn't, and his life has paid your passage out of here and the Royalists are none the wiser.

Philip stared northwards into the darkness. Somewhere out there was the woman he loved, the woman whose maidenhood he had taken, and whose love and trust he was about to grossly and vilely misuse. He could take the road to Aston Hall, the road to Lucinda. In doing so though, he would lose much more. Not simply his family, not merely his honour but something that was greater than both. Something intimately bound up with the burning houses of Birmingham, with the twisted body of a 14-year-old boy and especially with the brutal murder of this harmless lunatic.

Marriage to Lucinda would mark more than acceptance of this – he would be condoning it.

"Mr Roberts, sir? We should leave. The enemy may return and we'd be hard put to explain ourselves."

The enemy? Odd how quickly ambivalence can be forced to a decision. Yes, decision made and the last bridge burned. Now, come what may.

"Yes, you're right."

With a last glance at the body of the man whose unwitting sacrifice had saved them both, they mounted the horse and rode into the darkness.

"For what shall it profit a man, if he gain the whole world and suffer the loss of his soul?"

Neither looked back and only the crackling of flames pursued them.

When Miles Atkinson isn't teaching history and geography, he can usually be found reading about it. A life-long interest in the English Civil War and the Wars of the Roses has led him to take the first tentative steps in historical fiction – the first of which is this short story. He hopes it does justice to this little-known episode in Birmingham's history. Aside from writing, Miles is a member of the UK full-contact medieval combat team and competes at events across Europe.

The Regent

Lee Benson

To put it mildly, we are an eclectic group that meet up on a monthly basis to chat about anything but work. We call it the Cheapskates' Gathering.

We first met randomly one evening several months ago in a pub on Gas Street Basin and have continued meeting up ever since.

It's Anuska's turn to find somewhere.

"Where shall we go to eat?" she asks, not really knowing anywhere seeing as she's a newcomer to the city, studying hotel management at the college, and working somewhere off the canal basin at night to earn a few extra bob.

Pete the Feet pipes up. "I know a little French bistro in town off New Street and it's cheap as chips."

"I'm not a great lover of our city at night," I say. "Do we have to go into town?"

"Well it's easy to get there." Pete offers a good excuse. "It's only a few minutes' walk down past the town hall."

So I reluctantly agree. A quick shout out from those lovely people at WhatsApp and we total six.

We meet outside the bistro at seven. The building has an air of familiarity to it and I can't remember why as we go through a set of double doors and climb the stairs to a bit of a rundown wooden floor with cheap tables, benches and faded French posters.

Music plays through a tinny speaker stuck on the counter.

The French waitress, wearing ripped jeans and a tight white blouse, takes us to a long table.

157

"Use zis alf pleez," she says, and draws an imaginary line across the table surface.

Three of us have a bench and three are blessed with old school chairs.

She returns with cutlery and offers a choice of two starters: ham hock or green soup, followed by a cheese salad for veggies and chicken for those who aren't. Wine is simple: red or white. No expense spared here.

Brian is veggie and moans about his singular choice. Mind you, Brian has a tendency to moan at everything as his glass is always three quarters empty. Pete's a happy go lucky narrowboat mechanic. Zelda runs a boutique in Moseley. Anuska is a student. Colin is an art teacher in Wolverhampton and lives on a boat, and I'm a bit of a decorator.

The French bread and butter arrives in raffia baskets accompanied by three red and three white carafes of wine.

"Tuck in," says Colin. "I'm famished."

"I'll just wash my hands," I say, extracting my body from the hard bench and finding the sign for the *Gents.*

The loos are more like a cupboard, and there's a large hatch outside bearing a sign: *Forbidden – No Entry.*

Not just a plain *No Entry* sign. It intrigues me.

The owner of the place is talking to Pete. Steve is certainly not French, especially with his strong Geordie accent; however his wife is and she just bosses him around in the kitchen as he keeps telling us.

"Excuse me," I butt in. "I'm intrigued as to why there is a *Forbidden – No Entry* sign just outside the gents."

"Ah, it's the old lady's secret."

"Old lady?"

"Yes. This was the old exit to the cinema. The builders boarded it up years ago, made shop units on the front and the space lay dormant for years. We've rented a corner of it. Fancy a butchers?"

I knew it, we'd come up the side steps of a cinema.

"I'd love to."

"Anyone else want to tag along?" He lowers his voice and looks over his shoulder. "But you mustn't say a word. Insurance and all that."

The girls aren't interested and Brian shrugs his shoulders. "'I'll sit it out. Sounds messy to me."

Colin, Pete and I follow Steve. He picks up a chair and tells Pete to grab the torch from the desk/bar.

He unlocks the bolt. "Don't go too far. There's no flooring and it's a long drop down."

He helps us up while Pete turns the torch on and aims it into the dark.

There she is. I take in a great sigh.

The Regent.

My cinema from my childhood. A magical place of so much of my little life.

We look down and everything is covered in years of dust. The chairs are still there, so is the stage, although now a forlorn mess. There were 1200 seats in here, before it changed its name to the ABC New Street and finally closed in 1983. She's been locked away and forgotten from the heyday of cinema. Not like the massive 12-screen buildings you get now.

"Come on, you'll miss the start."

There's a man in a purple evening suit with matching bow tie. It's my uncle, holding out his hand for mine. The joy of seeing him again. He's a tall, proud man and the cinema manager.

I run as fast as my little legs will go to keep up with his giant strides and he sits me down on a red velvet chair.

"Stay here till the end. Vera will get you an ice cream, okay?"

I nod. "Thank you."

I wait for the film to start. I love coming to the cinema. My parents have dropped me off and will collect me later.

Every time, after the film finishes the usherette escorts me to the door marked with a gold star and *Manager* painted underneath: my uncle's office, full of posters and shelves of cinema memorabilia. I always feel very important waiting for my father to collect me.

This time I can sense the plush pile of the red velvet seat moving back and forth in my first two fingers, then the lights dim and the film begins.

It's my favourite actor. John Wayne. He's on his horse and part of the 7th Cavalry.

In the dark, I pick up the smell of popcorn. I'm transfixed. Vera brings me a vanilla ice cream tub with a wooden spoon and a tube of Smarties for being good.

More memories flood in.

He wasn't my real uncle. We always called grown-ups aunt and uncle. They lived a few doors down from us and my aunt always loved me. She told me so. She had only one daughter and always helped mom out taking me to the park.

I hear a rustle behind me.

It's the ticket lady in the foyer, surrounded by lots of shiny brass polished billboards. She's rather large and peers out of her glass-fronted kiosk. She presses buttons, which eject pink or purple tickets, smiling at me as I peer over her counter and says, "Come on! Your meal's going cold."

I blink. The dusty chairs are empty again.

Colin taps my shoulder. "What's got into you; you've not moved for ages?"

"I dunno," I say. "I wasn't here. Well I was, but a long time ago."

"It's that red wine, you plonker," he laughs.

We climb down through the hatch and rejoin the Cheapskates' Gathering.

"I used to come here when I was a lad. Looking at the old lady reminded me of so much."

"Like *déjà vu,* you mean?" asks Zelda.

"More like suddenly being back in time. It felt so real." I shrug.

"Rubbish," says Brian. "Don't believe in all that bollocks."

"Leave him alone," says Colin. "He stood totally still for bloody ages. I saw him. Didn't move an inch for ages."

"Wish *I* could go back in time. There's that bird I fancied a few months back. I'm sure I could have got me way."

We all laugh at Pete. He's one to bring everything back to basics.

"Maybe we should go to the pictures next time," says Anuska.

"Maybe. One things for certain, my old man won't be able to pick me up," I say, trying not to sound melancholic.

"Why not," says Anuska.

"He's been dead for over twenty years," I reply.

"Come on. Let's toast to the living," says Colin.

We settle up and leave. I hail a cab.

"Where to, guv?"

"Back in time, please."

"Sorry, mate?"

"Moseley village, thanks."

They were there. I know. I saw them all. My cinema, my folks, my uncle. My memories.

Till the next time, John Wayne.

Lee Benson loves playing the piano, painting in watercolours, photography and writing. He writes quirky humour, poetry and children's books. His second novel, Where's Your Art Gallery Now? *is not an instruction manual. Honest. Visit Amazon or* **andrewsparke.com** *for full list.*

Busking It!

Martin Tracey

Lance Maverick sprinted away from his pursuer, but the approaching tram threatened to trap him. A quick calculation found him gambling to run in its path as it crossed the junction of Corporation Street and New Street.

The tram driver sounded the horn as the seemingly crazy pedestrian just about avoided a collision with the huge bulk of metal, which served as Birmingham's latest transport system.

Maverick's gamble had forced his pursuer to halt her chase and wait until the tram passed by. Her name was Sabita and she stamped her foot in frustration before instinctively looking towards the area affectionately known by Brummies as 'The Ramp'. It seemed an age until she could begin her chase once more and Maverick had already passed the bookmakers and was heading towards the market stall, which specialised in handbags and belts. Sabita needed to move quickly. Soon her target would be lost amongst the bustling crowd in and around the Bull Ring. Spurred on by dogged determination she somehow found another gear and began to pick up pace. Desperate to gain ground, she had no time to concern herself with banging into the odd shopper as she weaved in and out. She barged into a tall chap, causing him to spill his bags of designer clothing. To be fair to Sabita, she did have the wherewithal to shout a very loud apology as she continued her chase.

Jody Roper, Premier League footballer for one of the Birmingham teams, and secret vampire-slayer, accepted the apology. It was not in his nature to stay angry for long and once he retrieved his bags from the floor he became totally enthralled in the chase before him.

Just as Maverick thought he could get away a figure stepped out of Union Passage, the inconspicuous opening on New Street that leads to the Britannia Hotel. Maverick's attempts at escape were suddenly in vain. He found himself halted by a full punch to the face, which floored him instantly. Maverick's attacker then swiftly followed up his assault with a sneaky but substantial kick to the ribs.

Even though he had looked pure evil in the eye and had slain vampires with his team-mates, Jody was still horrified at what he had witnessed. Realising that the woman who had collided with him and the attacker must be connected, Jody found himself also running to the scene driven by a mixture of concern and curiosity. As both Sabita and Jody reached the spectacle, a crowd of people were also beginning to gather. Unshaken but feeling inconvenienced by the gathering crowd, the attacker swiftly pulled out an ID badge and brusquely informed everyone to 'back off'. With Maverick still writhing on the floor in some considerable pain, Sabita was easily able to pull his arms around his back and place a pair of handcuffs tightly upon his wrists. The flashing of the badge had been enough for most people to comprehend the situation and either move away or continue to look on with a sense of fascination. Concern for the victim had all but evaporated once it had been realised that plain clothes detectives were now involved, but one voice in the crowd decided to challenge what was occurring.

"This is nothing short of police brutality."

"You're confusing me with someone who gives a shit, pal," said the plain-clothes detective who had dealt the blows.

"How dare you speak to me like that," said the stranger noticing the name on the badge was Judd Stone. "There are correct procedures for apprehending criminals and I'm sure what I have just witnessed isn't anywhere near. I have a good mind to report you to your superiors."

Stone was not impressed and easily irritated. Knowing that his colleague was now in charge of the situation, he moved confidently and deliberately towards the suited man who had dared to question his motives. Stone looked him straight in the eye.

"Is that right, Mr fucking do-gooder. Well before you think it's a good idea to go blabbing to whoever you think you should, let me tell you that this piece of shit lying on the floor has been supplying drugs to school kids, trafficking young girls from afar before pimping them out, probably to men like you, and is also suspected of multiple rapes. I'd say he's got off lightly so far, wouldn't you? Now I suggest you back off and keep your mouth shut before I really begin to lose my temper."

The 'do-gooder', who clearly felt intimidated, swallowed hard and simply nodded. In contrast, some of the crowd actually began to applaud Stone and there were cries of phrases such as 'he deserves what he gets' and 'lock him up and throw away the key'.

Two teenage girls were very taken indeed with the anti-hero cop, securing images of him on their mobile phone. One turned to the other to comment how much he reminded her of the actor Tom Hardy before they both burst into giggles.

Stone moved his attention back towards Maverick and ungraciously hoisted him to his feet by his hair. "Come on, Sab, let's take this lowlife off Birmingham's streets once and for all."

A police car then appeared and Maverick was placed in the car without contest before being driven away.

Throughout the drama, a beanie-hatted busker, her pitch in front of what was once the Yard of Ale pub, strummed her guitar. She belted out George Michael's *Freedom*, considering it comically ironic as Maverick was not going to have such a luxury anytime soon. There was however a double irony, for there was a worrying trend lately of buskers mysteriously going missing in and around New Street.

Jody was instantly drawn to her. Not just because he was a huge admirer of George Michael, but also because he found the busker's singing voice and stage presence, even on the cold pavement of New Street, enchantingly magnetic to him. As the busker finished the song, Jody placed down his bags and broke into a short burst of applause.

"Do you know any more George Michael songs?" he asked. The female busker radiated a cheeky smile and erupted into the iconic acoustic guitar riff of *Faith*. The performance soon transformed into a duo as Jody found himself singing along to the familiar lyrics. By the time the spontaneous pair had finished their performance, a crowd had gathered, cheering and clapping, followed by money clinking into a hat.

"Hey, you sing well for a footballer."

"Do I? So, you recognise me then?"

"Oh yeah, of course I do. It looks as though I'm not the only one either, seeing how my financial status has more than doubled on the basis of singing just one song with you."

Suddenly, the heavens opened over Birmingham causing the crowd to retreat to whatever shelter they could find.

"Come on, miss, let me treat you to a coffee. I'm sure you're due a break and I'd love to hear all about your musical influences."

The girl smiled her killer smile once more, gathered up her earnings and slung her beaten up guitar across her back. Jody reassembled his shopping bags and led the way.

Jody Roper had taken full advantage of his Saturday off. The team were the subject of the next televised Monday night football game so he had ventured into the city centre for some retail therapy – the team hadn't been performing too well lately and with Jody being the most experienced defender of the team, he had recently undergone a great deal of unwelcome scrutiny. He was pleased with the formal shirts he'd purchased in the Mailbox and also the latest available 80s compilation CD. In this day of downloads and streaming Jody still found pleasure in having a CD he could touch and feel. Jody always found great pleasure in reading the sleeve notes and analysing the song-writing credits of the artists. The fact that he already had in his possession every single track on this latest compilation was irrelevant to him. Jody loved the 1980s and it was only recently that he had opted for a contemporary haircut as opposed to his usual mullet cut.

Due to the heavy rainfall, the coffee shop had become busier than ever. Jody's slogan T-Shirt incorporating the bold lettering of 'CHOOSE LIFE' was wet through. The busker's beanie hat had slightly protected her hair from the driving rain. The wet wool felt uncomfortable against her head, so she removed it revealing her intensely coloured cherry-red hair in all its glory.

"Quick grab that table over there by the window, I'll bring the drinks over. My treat. What are you having?"

"Chai latte with soya milk, please," answered the grateful busker.

"Right you are. Do you want anything to eat?"

"No, I'm good thanks."

Jody watched from the queue as the busker sat down in her seat and placed her guitar on the chair opposite to save it for him.

Eventually, Jody was served and he walked over to join her, careful not to spill the drinks.

"One chai latte with soya for Madame and one americano for yours truly."

"Thanks, you're very kind."

"It's the least I could do after you played one of my favourite songs."

"Faith? It's a good song."

"Like a lot of songs from the 80s, it's my favourite era."

"I know that. That's how I recognised you. I don't know much about football to be honest but your love for 80s music has placed you in the spotlight quite a bit, Jody."

"So, you wouldn't know of any of my teammates?"

"I doubt it. Try me?"

"Charlie Cheng?"

"Nope."

"Bruiser Bradshaw?"

"Never heard of him?"

"I thought everyone knew Bruiser. How about Johnny Knox?"

"Oh, yeah I know him."

"That doesn't surprise me."

"He's quite a dish. A bit of a David Beckham character, isn't he? He's great at playing football but is also a marketing product in his own right."

"That's Johnny. More replica shirts are sold at the club shop with his name on the back than anyone else."

"Pass me my guitar."

Jody obliged.

"Here's one for Johnny Knox," said the busker and she cheekily performed the chorus of Carly Simon's *You're So Vain.*

The coffee shop occupiers applauded. It wasn't every day that they were subject to some light entertainment while they sipped their drinks.

"Johnny would see the funny side of that. He's a cool guy and a good friend. Play me another," said Jody.

"Okay, here's one of my own compositions. I'll just play you a couple of verses and the chorus."

Jody was in awe as the busker's beautiful singing voice entwined with her competent picking of the guitar strings. She was a very confident and capable performer. Her red hair which fell over her face as she played served to sharpen

Jody's focus on her gorgeous lips as they projected her thought-provoking lyrics.

More applause from the coffee shop attendees followed.

"That was fantastic. I really mean it," said Jody.

"Thanks."

"Perhaps you could run all your songs past me some time. I'd really like to hear them, you're really talented."

"Would you like your own private concert?"

Jody laughed. "I should be so lucky. So, who are your influences? I hear a bit of Lennon and Bowie in there perhaps?"

"Yeah, both those guys. I also like Jake Zennor and Blossom of Eden."

"Yeah, Zennor's good. Any 80s influences?"

"Definitely George. Consciously that's probably it for me though where the 80s are concerned. I mean outside of Wham! and the Faith album, a lot of George's material was in the 90s anyway."

Jody noticed her attention waver.

"What is it?"

"Look over there, it's those two plain clothes coppers from earlier."

"So, it is. I think they've earned a coffee break," said Jody.

The couple were surprised to find the detective known as Judd Stone approach them. "You're a busker, right?"

"That's right."

"Well I need you to be careful, Miss. We have had several buskers disappear from the city in the past few months."

"Really?" said Jody. "That is worrying."

"It certainly is and I wouldn't want this young lady to become the next missing musician."

"Thanks for the warning. I'll be careful," said the busker.

"Glad to hear it."

"By the way," said Jody, "for what it's worth I think you handled that situation perfectly well earlier. There's nothing wrong with dealing out a little poetic justice for scumbags like that. Take no notice of the do-gooder at the scene."

"Thank you. It's no good pussyfooting around with these types of people. You have to use language they understand and that's not necessarily a language of the spoken word."

"What my colleague means is that his style can be a little unconventional, but he gets results," added Sabita.

"I'll drink to that," said Jody taking a sip of his americano as if it was a toast of champagne.

"Come on, Sab," said Stone. "I can see a couple leaving a table over there, let's grab it. Quick. They're like gold dust in here."

As the two detectives bid farewell and ventured towards the vacant table, Judd Stone thought it obligatory to shout across the room. "And good luck for Monday night, Jody"

"Cheers."

Jody returned his attention to the busker. "That's really worrying about the buskers going missing round here. Why don't you try and find another patch to busk? There's always the High Streets at Harborne and Kings Heath for example."

"Not a chance. New Street is where I belong. Nothing could stop me performing here."

Jody was a little surprised by the determination in the busker's voice. "Do you know, I've spent all this time with you, heard you sing, shared a hot drink with you and I don't even know you're name?"

"It's Candy."

"Sweet as?"

"Sweet as."

"Please be careful, Candy. It would be a tragedy if something were to happen to you. You're clearly very talented and a lovely-natured girl."

"You don't know me that well. I may be a serial killer for all you know."

"Okay, so you're clearly very talented."

Jody and Candy both laughed.

"Thanks, it means a lot that you like my music. Clearly not everyone does or I'd have a record deal by now."

"Oh, you're good enough Candy, don't worry about that. The problem is the music industry is so fucked up these days. It seems to me that fat cat generated TV shows are the only avenue for any kind of recognition but if you don't fit their model, if you're not someone they can control, there's no hope. The nurturing of the artist is clearly at the back of the queue these days – it's all about making a fast buck where superficiality rules. Where is the avenue today for talented singer-songwriters with an air of originality like you? Look at the diversity of the 80s. We had Bowie, Culture Club, Duran, Frankie, Jacko, McCartney, Spandau, Wham!, Prince and Madonna all fighting for the number one spot and each of those artists were as original as they were gifted. They all had something different to offer but if any of them had relied on a TV show audition we probably would never have heard of half of them."

"I guess you're right. But you know what? I'm not exactly unhappy doing what I do. New Street is my concert venue."

"New Street it is then. But please, do be careful."

"Don't worry. I believe we all have angels that protect us."

"Oh really? You're quite spiritual then?"

"Yes I am. Spiritual but not religious. I believe that there are greater forces that control certain journeys and destinations that we encounter and there are things out there that we still can't explain. And when I'm playing my music I feel protected. I feel like I'm invincible and no-one and nothing can hurt me."

"That's really interesting, I feel like that when I'm playing football. Actually, I've researched a lot about the paranormal."

"Oh really, why's that?"

Jody hesitated in answering. He knew from first-hand experience that evil and supernatural activity was real. Once, he had almost been the victim of a blood-thirsty vampire, no less, and he and his teammates had even been responsible for destroying a bona fide nest of vampires, but he thought sharing this information with Candy would be a little too mind-blowing for her. He realised that telling his stories, as true as they were, could only sound like nonsense to most people so instead he provided a more conservative answer.

"Oh, you know, I'm just interested in that sort of thing. Always have been since seeing the Thriller video I guess."

"So, you believe in ghosts?"

"I do, yeah."

"Ghosts fascinate me. Ever seen one?"

"Not yet, but I'll be prepared when one does appear. Did you know that there are lots of different types of ghosts?"

"Really?"

"Oh yeah. They are nearly as diverse as the pop stars of the 1980s. You've heard of poltergeists, I'm sure?"

"I have," answered Candy attentively.

"Well they're the sort of ghost that create havoc. They will throw chairs across the room or make objects chillingly levitate. They find it amusing to make loud noises and they can even cause actual physical harm to humans by biting and hitting. Yet in contrast there are other ghosts that wish no harm at all. They can appear as clear as day, barely visible, invisible or perhaps translucent but are totally unable to make any kind of physical contact at all."

"Wow, that's really interesting."

"Then there are orbs, doppelgangers, demons, and do you know a ghost can even be conjured up?"

"Really? How can that happen?"

Jody found himself smiling at this turn of conversation. "How did we get onto this?"

"Go on, I'm really interested in the occult."

"Well this type of ghost is known as the artificial ghost. The artificial ghost is created from the art of psychokinesis. The most famous case was when a ghost called Philip was conjured up in Canada."

"Philip? Blimey if I was going to conjure up a ghost I'd give it a cooler name than Philip. I mean Philip is okay for a teacher or professor perhaps, but not for a ghost."

"A psychical research group in Toronto created him. Whole books have been written on their experiences with Philip. They then went on to create a Canadian spy called Lilith and a medieval alchemist called Sebastian."

"Lilith and Sebastian. Much better names than Philip for a ghost."

"Agreed."

"So how is it done?"

"People get together and combine their mental and spiritual energies. They decide beforehand on what sort of spirit they want to conjure up and then they join hands and concentrate on making the artificial ghost appear. They may also choose to use something like a Ouija board to gain a connection."

"That sounds awesome. I wanna do it."

"I'm not sure, Candy. It could be dangerous."

"No, it won't. It'll be fun. Come on, let's do it right here and now." Candy's enthusiasm was almost tangible.

"I'm not sure it's the right environment."

"Look Jody, we have only known each other for a small amount of time but would you agree we have made a connection, and one that's perhaps even a spiritual connection?"

"I can't deny that Candy. I feel very comfortable with you."

"And you like my music."

"And I like your music."

"Music is the single most effective powerhouse to connect people and transcend them to someplace else. So, come on, between us we can make this work. Let's do it. Take my hands."

"I still doubt it'll work in a bustling coffee shop but okay, if it means that much to you. So, what are the characteristics of our ghost going to be?"

"Err, we need some inspiration. Think of your love for 80s music."

"You spoke about the concept of angels offering protection. Wouldn't it be great if we could produce a ghost that could offer protection? I remember George Michael appearing in an American TV series called *Eli Stone* and the protagonist suffered hallucinations including seeing George appear as a guardian angel. I am not suggesting that I would want to conjure up George, rest his soul, but how's about our ghost could wear a cool biker jacket like George wore during the Faith era?"

"Yeah, why not? It was a great jacket. It had Rockers Revenge written on it as I recall."

"That's the one."

"We want our ghost to look good. How about the face not representing any specific gender? Keeping with your 80s theme, the ghost could have a pretty made-up face like Boy George used to."

"Okay, why not? And this ghost, if it appears, will have the power to protect?"

"Yeah. It'll have super-hero powers."

"It may as well be useful. Our very own super-hero, no less."

"That's so cool. What shall we call the ghost? Something better than Philip, I hope."

"Stan Trewee."

"Stan Trewee?" Candy screwed up her face in bewilderment. "What sort of a name is that? It doesn't strike me as the name of a super-hero ghost."

"Well, I've added in an 'a' but apart from that the name is made from an anagram of 'New Street'."

"Oh ok, that's very clever. Stan Trewee it is then. But I guess that sends the gender-neutral theory up in smoke."

"Not necessarily. You've seen the *Scream* films, right?"

"Yeah, I love 'em."

"What is the name of the lead female in *Scream*?"

"Sidney."

"There you go then. A traditional male name taken on by an all-American girl."

"Point taken. Our ghost is going to be very twenty-first century."

"Right then, Candy, now we kind of know what our ghost is to be it's time to join our hands and we will conjure up the all-protecting spirt of Stan Trewee." Jody paused realising he was perhaps getting slightly carried away. He was concerned for Candy more than anything – what if they did manage to conjure up a spirit against all the odds? "Wait, are you sure you want to do this? It really could be dangerous you know?"

"You bet I do. Don't worry I'm not scared of dead people. I've seen plenty before." Candy was excited beyond belief. She clearly believed that this was going to work. "Wait I have something that may give us a better chance."

Jody was puzzled as Candy reached into her bag and revealed a long rectangular box.

"What do you have there?" he enquired.

"Incense sticks. I'm sure I've heard that incense can be used in the process of evocation."

"Mmmm, I'm not so sure. I don't think the coffee shop manager will be too impressed with the smell of hippy overpowering the aroma of coffee, let alone the fire hazard."

"Okay, point taken." Reluctantly, Candy returned the box of sticks to her bag.

"I hope this still works. Ready, Jody."

"Ready."

Naively, the newly found friends joined hands and closed their eyes. As the seconds passed, they became engaged in a mutual trance-like state and although oblivious to their surroundings, Jody had enough presence of mind to call upon their potential creation through the power of whisper. Inevitably however, they were becoming noticed even though the coffee shop had emptied out a little. Eventually, their eyes opened in unison.

"Did you feel anything?" asked Candy.

"Nothing," answered Jody, amazed at his own level of disappointment at the lack of result. Had he really expected the experiment to work? "How about you?"

"No nothing."

Jody looked at his watch. "Blimey is that really the time? I should be moving on. I just to pop to the Gents first."

"That's a shame, we were having such a good time."

"I agree. I've really enjoyed your company, Candy. I'll come and check on you busking again."

Candy watched Jody walk towards the bathroom. She liked the way he walked. While he was gone she had a rummage around in her bag.

"I'm back."

"So I see. Aren't you going to finish your coffee before you go?" asked Candy.

"Yep," and with that Jody swigged down the last few mouthfuls of his lukewarm beverage. "Urggh, that lost its nice flavour quickly. How was the chai latte?"

"Good, thanks," answered Candy. "Come on then, time to go."

"I'm glad to see it's stopped raining," said Jody as they stepped outside. "Wooahh."

"Are you okay?" enquired Candy.

"Yeah, I just went a little dizzy all of a sudden. It must be the change of air." As soon as Jody had finished speaking he felt dizzy once again. There was no doubt about it, Jody Roper was feeling very strange indeed. He began to concern himself that he was being punished for his dabbling in the spirit world and had perhaps conjured up an unwanted entity that had decided to enter his body.

"It's okay, Jody. I'll take care of you." The striking face of Candy began to blur and fade as her words tailed off into oblivion.

♦

When Jody Roper woke, he found himself to be in complete darkness. The air felt cold and damp, yet he could sense he wasn't outdoors. His instinct was to try and move but something he took to be strap-like was preventing his legs and arms from moving. Then suddenly bright lights appeared all around, and he discovered that he was strapped to a chair. As he looked ahead, the beams dazzled his eyes. Then they dimmed, easing his temporary blindness. He could see before him what appeared to be a platform and then as his eyes adjusted to the environment, he realised the platform was in fact a stage. He knew this because there was a series of guitar amplifiers and a drumkit and a keyboard upon it. And propped against the drumkit and keyboard were what he took to be the musicians of these instruments, but shockingly their rotting state indicated that they were clearly dead.

In a new state of panic, Jody tried to free himself once more from the chair but his efforts were in vain as the straps were much too tight and secure. He was going nowhere.

Then he spotted a skeleton sitting on a chair with a bass guitar positioned across its lap and a guitar strap across its bony shoulder. At this point Jody felt compelled to let out a scream followed by frantic shouts of help.

Then the star attraction entered centre stage purely for Jody's entertainment. There was a slight feedback on the microphone as Candy began to speak. "Jody Roper, are you ready for your very own special concert? With the help of my band I'm going to play all of your favourite songs from the 1980s and of course a variety of my own music which you so kindly took an interest in."

"Where are we?" demanded Jody.

"This concert venue has been specially chosen for you, Jody. No one will disturb us as I perform my music to you. Actually, we are in very familiar surroundings. Can you guess where we are?"

"No," answered Jody incredulously.

"We are beneath New Street. The street where we first met. Did you know that there are many disused tunnels underneath Birmingham's city centre? We are in a very secret room just off the tunnel once used by the postal services that linked the former Royal Mail offices and New Street train station. Of course, now that the offices have been transformed into a stylish shopping and eating complex the tunnel is no longer used. Except by me that is."

"Your band. They're the missing buskers, aren't they?"

"They play to my tune, Jody. There's only room for one musician on New Street and that's me."

"You're fucking insane."

"Well that's gratitude for you. I'm about to perform to you your very own bespoke concert and you repay me by insulting me, Jody. I'm very disappointed."

"You drugged my coffee when I went to the Gents, didn't you?"

"Jody, it's time to be quiet, sit back and enjoy the concert."

"And what will you do with me once the concert has finished? Am I to end up like one of your band members?"

"Don't worry about that for now, Jody. Just sit back and get lost in the music. That's what I intend to do for the next hour or so."

Candy had switched from her acoustic guitar to an electric one and her opening chord bounced around the underground walls like an audible rubber ball. If it wasn't for his current acute state of fear Jody would have appreciated the sound in the underground site and even contemplated if this was how the music in The Cavern might have sounded when the Beatles were plying their trade.

Jody hung his head in desperation. He looked at his T-shirt which projected the slogan 'CHOOSE LIFE'. If he could, he would, but he wasn't convinced it was his choice to make anymore. How he wished he could get in touch with his buddies from the football team, the same buddies who he had stood side-by side with to defeat a nest of vicious vampires.

He wished he could somehow get in touch with that uncompromising cop too. What was his name? Judd Stone? He would get him out of this trouble for sure.

Jody raised his head to see Candy strutting about the stage. She was crazy but boy was she talented. But what was to become of him once the music was over? Jody was really concerned about his safety and also his destiny.

Then just behind Candy something began to take form from out of nowhere.

Jody widened his eyes and dared to hope as a leather jacket with the words 'Rockers Revenge' slowly began to appear.

Martin Tracey is an author who pushes the boundaries of reality. The supernatural and thought-provoking elements that cut through his stories take you on a journey of thrills and suspense but remain believable. He's a down-to-earth author who likes to champion his beloved Birmingham. You can read more about the characters featured in this short story in the following Martin Tracey publications: Jody Roper, Johnny Knox: Beneath The Floodlights. *Judd Stone, Sabita Mistry:* Mind Guerrilla; Club 27. *Jake Zennor:* Things They'll Never See. *Find out more at* **martintracey.co.uk**.

Buffalo Bill and the Peaky Blinders

Andy Conway

"We'd like you to meet Buffalo Bill on New Street."

This was how I began my search for Katherine Bright: sitting in the Moseley apartment above Mrs Hudson's costume hire shop.

It was 1976 for me, but Mrs Hudson and Mitch were visiting from 2017. We would occupy this same two-storey flat above the shop at various times. Having a physical location that remained a constant between us somehow made the travelling through time thing easier.

But you never knew when someone was going to drop in.

I stared at the photograph Mrs Hudson had put in my hands.

Native Americans riding down New Street. It was quite a sight. I knew the story. I'd seen the photograph before. The paper had run an 80-year anniversary special on it a while back. Buffalo Bill bringing his *Wild West* show to Birmingham for the first time, with a hundred Native Americans in full regalia riding painted horses down New Street, watched by a sea of startled locals.

The locals were almost as fascinating as the Indians. A huddle of Victorians gazing up at the warrior braves riding by. A man with a grey beard carrying a Gladstone bag, a young gent in a straw boater, a woman in a black dress and bonnet, a gaggle of young boys in shabby suits and flat cloth caps. Little Peaky Blinders.

"November third, 1887, to be exact," she said.

"It should be easy," said Mitch.

I looked up from the photo to meet Mitch's eyes, but found myself staring at his waxed moustache. Was this a look he'd adopted to travel back to Victorian Britain with me or was it the fashion in 2017, forty years from now?

"I've never gone that far before," I said. "You know that."

I'd been their mid-century man for almost ten years now, after stumbling across their time travel activities in '66. The sixties and seventies were easy to me, even the fifties were a doddle. I'd gone as far back as '46, the year I was born, but no matter how exciting it was, I wanted to stay right here, with my wife and my daughter.

"You need to get over this block you have," said Mitch. "It's perfectly easy to travel outside your own lifetime. We've all done it. I'm doing it now."

"You're not born yet?" I tried not to sound surprised; it was just he looked and dressed like my great granddad.

"I'm born next year," he said. "But I've gone back to the thirties, and even further."

"So why me? Why don't *you* go and get her?"

They exchanged an awkward glance.

"We think she might recognise us," Mrs Hudson said.

"She'll recognise me too," I said. "She broke my bloody camera."

"We think she'll probably not remember most of what happened. Amnesia is a feature of the, er, process she's been through. But she's more likely to remember us than you."

"And why's that?" There was something they weren't telling me. "What did you do to her?"

That look between them again.

Mitch leaned forward.

"Do you love your wife, Pete?"

"Course I do. What's that got to do with anything?"

"And your child?"

"Are you taking the Mick? 'Course I love my daughter."

"That's why you're the best for this. Newly married, a lovely daughter. You've got a lot to hang onto."

"Good reasons for not travelling to a place I don't know. A place that's risky."

"The thing about Katherine," Mrs Hudson said, soothingly. "Is that she can have an adverse effect on the minds of men who come into contact with her."

"What do you mean?"

"She's a succubus," said Mitch. "She will seduce you, use you for her own ends and devour you."

"We don't know that," laughed Mrs Hudson. "Mitch has some rather extreme theories on the matter, but she has led at least one man astray, and her own poor self, I might add. But we have no idea if that's still a part of her, or if she presents any danger whatsoever. That's what we'd like you to find out."

"So you need a happy family man? Someone who won't be tempted."

"Plus she smashed your camera," said Mitch. "So you probably hate her."

I remembered the girl. Flowing red hair, bright green eyes. She was staying in this same flat in '66, on a mission they'd given her. I'd never seen her since then, even though she was part of their time travelling cabal.

"You need to tell me what happened to her," I said.

Mitch opened his leather satchel and pulled out a file. "Everything is here."

Inside was a sheaf of dense type, a wad of Victorian banknotes, a letter, and a few printed calling cards bearing my name: *Peter Wethers, Esq.*

"All you have to do," said Mrs Hudson, "is use the letters of introduction to get yourself attached to Buffalo Bill's tour as a reporter, and then talk to her. Make an assessment of her psychological profile."

"Her what?"

"Find out if she's still crazy," said Mitch.

"But really, it's very simple. Get yourself into Buffalo Bill's circle and it's mission accomplished."

The door sounded downstairs and Sandra called up, back from the shops with the baby, the cold air on their cheeks. I felt a flush of love and a desire to go down and hug them, soak up that feeling.

Mitch was right. I hadn't thought about another woman in two years. I'd stopped noticing them. I'd be ideal.

Damn.

"We'll go," said Mrs Hudson. "Good luck."

I walked out, leaving them in the upstairs back room that was my studio and darkroom, knowing they'd be back in their own time before I'd got downstairs and kissed my little girl.

♦

I hung on for a few days. It didn't matter when I chose to go – 1887 would always be there – but I realised I was putting it off. The idea scared me. I wanted to hang onto *now*, this perfect life I had. It didn't matter that I could go and spend a month in 1887 if I liked and come back to the exact same minute I'd left. My wife and my daughter might not miss me. But I'd miss them.

So, I read through the file, counted the money, readied my Victorian clothes and studied a map of the city centre from about the same time.

I've always liked a good western, I was brought up on them at the Saturday cinema club, but the films that came out recently knocked me sideways. I watched *Little Big Man* and I never heard General Custer's *Garryowen* tune again without thinking of massacred Indians. I watched *Soldier Blue* and puked up. I could never again watch a western without feeling sorry for the Indians and what was done to them. And it didn't surprise me when they protested all over again a few years ago at Wounded Knee. If I were one of them I'd be raging my whole life.

And I was going to see some real Natives. And Buffalo Bill too. The man himself.

I left Sandra sleeping one night, kissed the baby in her cot, sneaked across the landing to my studio – the one room in the house that was off limits to my wife and child – and put on my Victorian clothes, pocketed the money, the letters, the calling cards. I sat in the comfy chair and tried to relax and remember exactly how I'd felt all the other times.

My eye roamed the photo again. The photographer had stationed himself on New Street, at about where they would later build The Ramp, to catch the procession as it passed. But what he'd captured – and this was what really fascinated me, as a photographer myself – was a culture clash. The Indians of the Plains, only eleven years after the Battle of the Little Big Horn, and still two years before the Wounded Knee massacre and the death of Sitting Bull, riding down a street of English Victorians.

I realized the photographer could have achieved a more interesting shot if he'd placed himself higher up and pointed his camera straight up the street, to capture how long the parade was. With over two hundred performers, half of them Indians, it would have stretched the entire length of New Street and he might have captured it snaking right up to the vanishing point of the Town Hall building.

But he'd chosen to point his camera at an angle, to capture that corner and its pavement, with its cluster of startled locals.

It was these choices a photographer made that interested me. And back then the photographer was surely working with plates, having to replace them one by one. Each would take a minute to load and unload as that procession sped past. This was why there was just a single shot of Buffalo Bill riding by in an open carriage, and two shots of the Indians.

None of the Indian women.

And this was a problem. Because it was one of those women I had to find.

It wasn't working. I was still sitting in my flat in 1976, eyes burning, head pounding, and all I could do was fall asleep.

I woke up angry. It was hopeless. 1887 was too far away to imagine. There was too much of a gulf between me now and that time for me to believe I could do it.

Maybe it was that I didn't want to do it anyway.

I wrote down my failure on an index card, noting the exact time and date, lifted the framed photograph of Moseley village in 1879 from the wall and opened the safe behind it. Inside was the old cigar box. Twenty or more small envelopes, musty and yellowing, each labelled with a single name: *Abshire, Bailey, Collier, DeTamble, Eakins, Foster...*

I had no idea what the names meant, but I knew that each envelope represented a mission. I ignored the rest, as instructed, put my message in *Morley* and placed it back in the safe.

Half an hour later, Mitch appeared in the room. He looked dead beat, frayed at the edges, his eyes red-rimmed. Whatever was happening in 2017 it wasn't good. But then, I remembered, Mitch was an empath. It was emotions that he soaked up. Maybe he was feeling my hopelessness. Feeling it more than I felt it. I tried to imagine him in this same room, forty years in the future, opening the safe every day, opening the *Morley* envelope to see what was written inside. Thinking himself back to this time. *Feeling* himself back to this time. All time was happening at the same moment. Once you realised that, it made travelling through time so much easier. But it was a terrifying thought.

"I can't get through," I said. "Something's stopping me."

"Perhaps you should go stand at New Street, in the same spot. Maybe that will make it easier."

I shook my head. "It looks nothing like it does in the photograph. Horrible busy intersection now, clogged with traffic. You can't see the street through the buses and exhaust fumes."

He paced, twirling his silly waxed moustache points for a while.

"You're a photographer," he said. "You think in visual terms. I thought the photograph would work."

"It usually does."

"I think I have an idea. But you're going to have to come to our time."

"The future?"

I couldn't imagine being in the twenty-first century. 2017 was a date they only had in science fiction stories. I'd seen *2001: A Space Odyssey* at the Gaumont. Would 2017 be like that: all space stations and rocket launches? In forty years, I'd be in my seventies. I couldn't imagine being forty, let alone seventy. Mrs Hudson and Mitch had never given me any hint that I was still alive in their time. I assumed I wasn't.

Because if I was alive in their time, wouldn't they be asking my older self?

"There's a new invention," he said. "It might freak you out a bit, but it might be just the thing we need."

"Is it a time machine?" I joked.

"You could call it that," he said.

◆

A tram.

They had trams back in the city. These were not like the trams of my childhood – rattling charabancs dragged by the net of electric cables that smothered every street, the trams they'd torn out after the war and replaced with fume-belching buses – these were smooth gliding sleek bullets, exactly the kind of thing I expected of the future.

The tram ran along Stephenson Street and turned up the hill to Corporation Street, crossing that intersection with New Street where Victorians had stood amazed watching Sioux Indians a hundred years before.

No. A hundred and *forty* years ago.

I couldn't help peering through the windows to see how the city had changed. New Street was now pedestrianised – imagine! There was a new station building all made of shiny chrome. And the people walked around looking at pocket calculators.

Mitch chattered, distracting me as if he didn't want me to look too closely. Maybe he thought it would divert me from the mission.

The tram rode right up Corporation Street and I noticed new shops made of glass. Something called *Poundland*. Quite a few shops boarded up. They were either closed or this was some new anonymous retail fashion. We turned into Bull Street and there were more glass towers squeezed between the buildings I knew. It knocked me off balance.

The Gaumont cinema was gone. I got a flash of Colmore Row and Snow Hill station, but it was nothing like the station I knew. The old Edwardian building they were knocking down in 1976 was now a vast concrete plaza edged with glass buildings. Did they not build anything with stone anymore?

Then we were gliding down a canyon between two great buildings with a grass verge to the side.

"Are you all right?" Mitch asked.

I was standing with my palm covering my eyes, staring at my Edwardian shoes.

"I feel a bit dizzy."

"Just don't look at it, if it bothers you."

We shuddered to a halt and stepped off onto a platform. I raised my head and took it all in. A dirty collection of platforms not too dissimilar to the old Victorian station I knew. We stepped to the side and joined a crowd of people. I was thinking how we both might look out of place in our old-fashioned clothes but it seemed everyone around us was in Victorian garb. It really had come back into fashion.

I gripped my raincoat over my arm, like it was a lifebelt, swiped my straw boater from my head and wiped my sweating brow with my cuff.

Mitch patted me on the back. "It'll be here in a minute."

I nodded, like I understood, concentrating very hard on not falling over. Deep breaths. Sucking up fresh, cold air into my lungs.

A tram came in the opposite direction, triggering a chatter of excitement from the crowd around us. We stepped on board and huddled into a corner seat at the rear where we could see the backs of everyone's heads. They were all dressed in Victorian clothes too. Had those fashions come back or were they sightseeing time travellers like me? Lots of derby hats, a straw boater like mine, a few top hats, some flat caps. Lots of shouting and laughing. A party atmosphere.

The tannoy chimed and a pleasant female voiced said, *"Welcome to the Virtual Reality Tour of Birmingham."*

"What's that?" I whispered.

"You'll see."

The tram set off back the way we'd come and a few people cheered further down. I felt us rising, and suddenly the windows lit up.

"Sit back and take in the sights of Birmingham as it was in the past."

"What *is* this?"

Mitch patted my arm. "Don't worry, it's just a visual display in three dimensions. It's made to match where we're riding. We're going to see a simulation of the city as it was in the Victorian era."

So this was his new time machine: an amusement park ride.

We came up onto Bull Street and through the windows there were no glass buildings, no cars, buses, no people staring at their pocket calculators – just sepia brown streets crowded with horses and carts, the pavements alive with Victorians. Some of them seemed unreal, like cartoons. Others looked like they from an old film.

Now it made sense, the crowd on the tram was a fancy dress party, taking a tour into the past.

"Concentrate," said Mitch. "When we pass New Street, that's your moment."

I nodded, dug in my pocket and pulled out the photograph. Native Americans riding past the corner of New Street and Corporation Street.

The woman on the tannoy intoned a soothing commentary about our surroundings but I tried to shut her out. We were sliding down Corporation Street. A horse and cart rode alongside us for a while till we left it behind.

"See it," said Mitch. "Feel yourself back in that time."

The photograph in my hand. The Victorian street racing by. *The fourth of November, 1887,* I thought. It was racing towards me. I wanted to close my eyes to concentrate but I forced them open, staring, drinking it in, trying not to blink.

We dipped down the slope and I could see it ahead, the intersection with New Street.

Mitch took his hand from my arm, releasing me – *unanchoring* me. The corner of the street rushed towards me and I turned to my right to catch it.

On the curve of the corner, the shop sign *H. Greaves* with its sloping blind, and next to it *Cornish.*

There.

Dizzy.

Falling.

My eardrums burst and I tasted tin on my tongue, like I'd been punched. A cold blast of air.

Lying on the street. My hands grazed.

"Here, what the blazes!"

Rough hands dragging me up. A policeman. Walrus moustache.

"You'll get yourself ruddy killed falling here!"

Pulling me out of the street to the corner. A boy darted past to pick something up.

"Oy!" yelled the policeman. He slapped the boy round the ear and took the thing he'd snatched from the street. Handed it to me.

"Here you are, sir." His eyes bugged out as he saw it.

My roll of banknotes.

"You nearly lost that, sir."

"Thank you," I croaked, shoving it into my pocket.

"Now stand well back."

I could see the boy, a shabby-suited, flat-capped ragamuffin, rubbing his ear and scowling on the corner of New Street and Corporation Street, under the blind and the shop sign that said *36. H Greaves.*

Another policeman on the other side, pushing people back, bodies standing in the street the pavement was so narrow.

A gang of boys over there. A man with a grey beard and a Gladstone bag. I looked at the photograph in my hand.

The same scene. The only thing missing was the Indians riding by. And the young chap in the light suit and straw boater. I glanced around to find him, expecting to see him joining the tableau.

The photographer was directly in front of me, bending over his box on a tripod, loading a plate, covering his head with a black blanket.

Hysterical laughter fizzed in my throat. Standing behind him, holding the photograph he was about to take. These moments of time never to be repeated.

I was there. I'd done it. I was in 1887.

Catching my breath, trying to breathe deep and slow, knowing I'd faint if I didn't calm down. A sudden growling in my stomach. Ravenous hunger. I looked behind me. There was no ramp to the shopping centre. A great ornate building sloping down the hill of Stephenson Street. The old Exchange building. I'd almost forgotten it.

But I'd grown up with it there and seen it demolished ten years ago.

I felt sudden excitement. The urge to run around and drink it all in: the city as it used to be. Always this sensation. Always this need to close your eyes and count to twenty and tell yourself you're here for a reason, not your own curiosity.

But, oh God, it was such a beautifully grand Victorian city. And they'd just knocked down as many of the beautiful buildings they could and replaced them with Brutalist concrete. When you could go back and see it all like this, you realised what a crime it was.

It was cold. I felt it through my thin suit. Across the street, the straw boater man still hadn't arrived, and I could hear excitement up the street. The roar of the crowd far up there. The ringing of hooves echoing off the buildings.

Then I realised.

I pulled the photograph from my pocket to look closer.

The man in the summer suit and straw boater.

It was *me.*

I cried out with astonishment. All this time staring at the photograph and I hadn't recognised myself!

The procession was coming. A band blasting out a hideous brass cacophony. I had to get across the street. Get into the photograph.

The policeman was holding us back. I dodged him and ran across to the other corner and took my place beside the grey-bearded man with the Gladstone bag.

The cheers rippled through the crowd like a wave, just ahead of the open carriage that headed the procession, drawn by two white horses walking at a snail's pace. One man held the reins, with a top-hatted footman standing behind him.

The man driving the carriage wore a royal blue frock coat with a pale brown Stetson, and from under his white beard he smiled broadly, his eyes resting on me for a moment.

Buffalo Bill.

Behind him came a broad open wagon that housed the Cowboy Band, with their deafening brass fanfare. And then a long parade of cowboys on horseback. Some of them waved their pistols and rifles in the air. One of them spun a lasso above his head. That woman smiling benignly. Was she Annie Oakley?

After the cowboys came the Indians, led by one man imperious on a white horse, a handsome face with bright eyes that shone like sapphires, though they could not have been blue. He had the poise of royalty and everyone around me fell silent as he passed. This must have been Red Shirt, the chief who had so impressed Queen Victoria.

Then came the genuine Sioux Indians riding four abreast in their buckskin breeches and war shirts decorated with multicoloured quillwork, eagle-feathered war bonnets shining brightly above their heads.

And behind them the women. I scanned them for the face I might recognise. Somewhere in their midst was Katherine Bright, the woman I'd come to investigate.

A commotion.

A chestnut brown horse was skittish, panicking, and its rider was struggling to control it. Another Native woman struggled to reach over to pat the horse and hold its reins.

Her red hair, unmistakable, though she was dressed just like all the other Native women. She might easily pass for one of them if you hadn't expected to find her among them.

And. Oh.

She was beautiful.

Pity flooded my heart. She'd been banished, sent to a far-flung corner of the earth. She had suffered. She had crawled a million miles through dirt and pain.

I felt an overwhelming desire to help her.

And then she was gone and the parade was over, only a band of leafleters surging through the crowd pressing flyers into every hand. Buffalo Bill's *Wild West*. At Aston Lower Grounds. The first show starting tomorrow.

The people who'd been jammed against me now stepped into the street, dispersing. The photographer on the opposite corner packed away his camera, smiling to himself.

"This is him."

"This one, Herbie?"

I stumbled. Something knocked me hard.

The little boy with the cap. His friends surrounding me. I looked for the policeman, but he was far up New Street.

"What ya mean, stealing from our mate Herbie, here, eh, mister?"

The tallest of them, right in my face, a vicious snarl of hate. He could only have been twelve years old, they were all children, but violence came off them like the stink of beer.

"What do you mean?" I said, trying to raise my voice, to draw attention to what was happening. "I didn't touch him."

No one noticed. Was I invisible?

The tall boy shoved me in the chest again. "You took his money. You need to give it back."

"I didn't take anything. He tried to steal *my* money."

"Prove it," he spat. "Let's see it."

They were going to mug me. There was a razor in his hand. I hadn't seen him take it out. My throat clammed up. Fear and adrenalin flooding me.

I was too aware of the raincoat over my arm. I needed to free it, so I could punch. Then, like I hadn't made the decision myself, I threw it over his head.

And I was running down New Street, pushing and dodging through the crowds.

I'd punched him too. So fast I hadn't seen it myself. Thrown the raincoat over his head, punched him, and shoved them aside. A tangle of fallen bodies.

But they were behind me. Chasing me through the crowd. That I knew.

I didn't look back.

Tearing down New Street, aware that at the bottom I could turn right into the markets, or left onto the High Street.

There, a policeman up ahead. I could run to him. He would stop this.

Two men in cloth caps between him and me. Their eager eyes spotted me, saw prey, saw the commotion rolling through the crowd in my wake.

I sprinted right and found myself running down a steep hill. Not the street I'd expected to see. No, that street was built in the *sixties*. But there was no Rotunda now. No concrete underpass leading down to the markets.

Was this Spiceal Street? The spire of Saint Martin's the only thing I recognised down there. And the Nelson statue before it, in the middle of the street that widened out into a square. I ran down, past a pub called *The Lion & Lamb,* wild thoughts of taking sanctuary in the church.

The pavements alive with people. Flower girls in tattered shawls. Market traders. Bowler-hatted gentlemen. A few in top hats. Every shop had a blind drawn over the pavement. They screened me from my pursuers. But I heard them pounding behind me.

My ridiculous straw boater. A beacon, leading them to me. I thought of throwing it. But the summer jacket, just as bright and conspicuous. It made me a swimmer oozing blood in a sea of sharks.

Veering to the left, past Nelson. Not the church. God would offer no protection. A street to the left. *Moor Street.* I could hop on a train and escape? Glancing up, I recognised nothing. No station. Had it been built yet?

On, down the crowded pavement above which the street sign said *Bull Ring*. Lost. All of this was gone.

American Fresh Meat Company, Birmingham Coffee House, a hop merchants, a milliner, a chemist. Three golden balls hanging above the street, a pawnbroker.

None of these could offer me escape.

A baker's on the corner. An alleyway to the left, arched.

I ducked in and stopped short.

Golden Court.

A narrow, grimy alley of hovels. An old slum right in the city centre.

I pushed on, looking for a way out. Stinking, thick with human grime, dodging startled urchins in rags, old women and men huddled in the gloom like dazed opium smokers.

My chest burning, I nipped into a back yard, closing the gate behind me. No one in the yard. Laundry flapping on a line. The stench of ordure, cabbage and something rancid, something dead.

Doubled over, trying to breathe, I retched into my hand, dry heaving.

Footsteps gunning down the alley. Tearing past.

I crouched to my haunches. I didn't want to play anymore. I wanted to go home. I'd failed.

I could go home right now. Flit back in time. Go back to 1976.

Thinking hard, holding my breath, I wished myself back. I didn't want to be here, in this stinking cesspit, being hunted by psychopathic children. Home, with my wife, kissing the head of my beautiful daughter.

I thought of her, till I could almost smell her skin.

No good.

It wouldn't come. Fear could dampen the skill. This was why I needed photographs and images so much. I could focus on them and shut out everything else. If I'd brought a photograph of them with me – Sandra and the baby – I could get back to them.

Stupid stupid stupid!

I was stuck here.

More clomping boots down the alley, racing past the gate that hid me. Shouts and calls. They were all around.

I was trapped.

The gate creaked open. I looked up with fear, springing to my feet, ready to punch and kick and claw my way out of there, glancing around for a weapon, a stick or something.

A man staring at me, topless, his braces hanging from his trousers. Thick moustache.

Not the yard gate. The back door. He'd come out of his house.

Boots echoing down the alley again, coming back for me.

The man looked at me and I could see he was scared.

I put my finger to my lips.

He nodded. Then gestured me inside.

Voices clustering in the alley.

"He come in this way."

"He dain't come out ahead."

"He must be in one of these yards."

I walked to the man and rushed into the dark house. He followed and shut the door behind him.

Scared to breathe, I stood in the damp scullery. The man peeked through the dirty windowpane and I peered over his shoulder.

The yard gate creaked open. A child with a peaked cap peered in, looking the place up and down, then stared right at us.

But did not see.

He turned and closed the gate.

The man took my arm and ushered me through a grim kitchen to the next room. A young woman sitting before a meagre fire with a baby on her lap. She looked up with surprise.

Her husband reached for a shirt and pulled it on, strapping the braces over his shoulders.

"This gentleman was being chased," he said. "You're safe now."

I breathed again.

"Who was chasing him?" the woman said.

"Never you mind, Lizzie."

"I said *who,* Edward?" Then she looked up to me, as if in apology. "We don't want no trouble, sir."

"I didn't mean to bring you any, madam," I said, and swiped the boater off my head.

She laughed a little and I wondered if calling her *madam* was the wrong thing to say, but I could see Edward smiling too.

"You're not quite dressed for the weather, sir," he said. "No wonder the Peakies picked you out."

Lizzie clutched her throat and held the baby closer to her breast. "The Peakies?" she whispered. "We don't need Wellie Davies coming here killing us!"

Tears had sprung to her face and Edward rushed over to stroke her arm.

"It's all right. Don't you fret, sweetness. Wellie Davis ain't coming here."

"I'm sorry," I said. "I'll go."

I moved to walk back out to the yard. It didn't matter how many kids with razors were waiting for me out there, I couldn't bear the thought of making this woman cry.

Edward pulled me back. "You go out there, you're a dead man. You just sit over here for a bit."

He pushed me onto a rickety wooden chair next to the table.

"Lizzie. Some tea for our guest."

She nodded, wiped her face and humped the baby into his arms. "I do apologise, sir."

I sat with my straw boater on my lap, took a white handkerchief from my summer suit jacket pocket and mopped the sweat from my face.

Lizzie was bustling in the cramped kitchen, lighting a fire under a kettle, and I watched Edward bouncing the baby on his knee, grinning contentedly to himself. For a while he said nothing to me, and I let my gaze roam over the room, taking stock of how poor this young couple were, and yet how happy. Destitution had not yet worn them down, as it surely would, sometime soon. No matter how much they loved each other and their child, poverty would break in and kill their dreams.

The baby coughed as if to confirm my dark thoughts. Would it even survive another year in this slum? I'd seen the startling figures for this kind of place at this time in history: fifty-five percent of children died before they reached the age of five years. This baby had less than half a chance of making it. Death would run amok through this row of shabby dwellings and take every other child. Would it be this one?

Edward rocked it on his chest and whispered to it, soothing, gentle. "There now, sweet Emily," he said.

A girl. Just like mine.

I thought of the poverty Sandra and I had suffered when we'd tried to set up our own home. It was nothing compared to this, but that grubby bedsit in Erdington, and the baby on the way, and no money, and the nights I lay awake in bed wondering how I was going to look after a wife and a child when I was just a boy who could barely look after himself. The terror of it. And some nights the blind fear that made me want to run away. And then it had all been resolved, with Mrs Hudson. *You can live in the flat above my shop, rent free. It's two floors, two up, two down, almost the size of a house.* The relief. Like being dug out of a collapsed building and feeling daylight on your face. Sun and air rushing into you. Hope.

I watched Edward hold his coughing baby girl as if his arms could protect her from the poverty that was already inside her. A kind man. As if I didn't already know it.

When he looked up at me and smiled nervously, I found myself saying, "Do you still have your wedding suit?"

♦

The tea was weak and insipid, but it cheered me up.

"This is for your suit," I said, taking half of the notes from the roll and laying them on the table.

Lizzie clutched her throat again, wide-eyed, her cheeks flushing scarlet. Edward almost dropped the baby.

"It's too much," he said.

"We don't accept charity, sir," said Lizzie.

"Then please accept my gratitude. You saved my life. And my life is worth a lot more than this."

They looked at each other for a long moment, then nodded.

I went to the front room where their bed and the child's cot were crammed side by side, realising they only had the ground floor rooms and there was probably another family or two upstairs. I'd imagined Death coming and calling at every second house for a child, but the grim fact was that he would call at every single damp hovel and take one or two of them.

But not this one. Not this child.

I'd seen the hope on their faces. That pile of notes meant medicine they couldn't otherwise afford, food, nutrition, even a way out of this slum.

Edward's suit was a tight fit, but it looked decent. I pushed my remaining banknotes, photographs, calling cards, notebook and such into the pockets.

When I came back to the parlour Lizzie nodded her approval, and Edward handed me his best derby hat.

"Much better," he said. "If I say so myself."

"I'll look like every other man now," I said. "You can keep my suit and boater."

"Don't think I'll find much use to wear that kind of–"

Lizzie shushed him. "You're very kind. He'll look grand in it next summer."

I guessed she would sell it, and I didn't mind. I thought of the relief when Mrs Hudson had offered me the flat above the shop. If you could bottle that feeling it would be sweeter than champagne.

"I can't thank you enough," I said.

"You've thanked us more than enough," said Edward.

"You've changed our lives," said Lizzie, and she rushed forward and kissed my cheek, then retreated and stared at the threadbare rug, blushing.

Edward only smiled and patted me on the arm. "Come. Let's go."

He put on his coat and a derby that had seen much better days and led me through to the front door. We stepped into a courtyard that seemed to be a workshop premises. *Phoenix Works, Harness Furniture*, a painted sign said, the place thick with smoke from a fire somewhere. The stench of the street caught in my throat again.

"This way," he murmured.

We walked through the courtyard and along an arched alleyway, out onto the street. Park Road. Edward turned right and we walked swiftly, just two men off to the pub or the evening shift, heads down.

On the other side of the road, a building I recognised. The familiar gloomy frontage of the place they called *the Mucker*. The sign above the door said *The London Museum Concert Hall*. In my time, a nightclub and karate centre.

Boys in peaked caps skulked around one of the entrances. Were they the same boys who'd chased me? They noticed us. Looked a little too closely.

"Keep walking," Edward hissed. 'That place is a Peaky hangout.'

We walked on up to St. Martin's.

A shout behind.

'Let's run,' I said.

Edward gripped my hand. 'Easy.'

A cabstand opposite, under the shadow of the church. Could we hop on and speed off in time?

We turned the corner, not looking back, and there was the hill I'd run down earlier. Spiceal Street. The shopkeepers pushing the blinds back, market traders packing up in the failing light. We marched up the hill past Nelson and *The Lion & Lamb* till we turned into New Street.

Edward stopped at a line of cabs.

"You'll get a man to take you to Aston here."

I thanked him, feeling guilty that I had no intention of going to Aston to see Buffalo Bill. Once Edward was gone, I would think myself back home to my baby girl. They could go and whistle for their mission. There was nothing more important than family.

But Edward wouldn't hear of leaving me there. He waited until I was sitting up in a jarvey and he'd instructed the cabman to take me to Aston Lower Grounds.

"Buffalo Bill. I'd love to go and see that," he said. Then he laughed, as if at a happy memory. "You know. We *will* go and see it. It's a once in a lifetime opportunity."

I smiled and waved as the cab pulled off.

Of course. He could afford to go and see it now. He could afford more things than he'd ever dreamed he could. A stranger had walked into his back yard and opened up a world of possibility to him. *Life.*

The cab thundered up New Street where cowboys and Indians had ridden only hours ago and I patted my pockets. The roll of money, my notebook, calling cards, a letter of introduction to Colonel W.F. Cody, otherwise known as Buffalo Bill, informing him I was a reporter from *The Birmingham Daily Post* assigned to write a story about his famous show. It would get me inside the camp and afford me an introduction to his Native American translator, a certain Katherine Bright.

Pity swelled in me again. That poor woman. What had she been through? Pity and something else. A warmth in my chest that made me smile stupidly.

An old man was lighting the lamps up New Street and one of them caught the outline of a walking figure, hunched over, a peaked cap.

The cab swerved away and thundered up Corporation Street and I thought of my baby girl, sleeping safe at home, some night one hundred and twenty years from now.

She was safe.

I would go ahead with my mission and get back to her and she would never know I'd been gone.

I shivered, but not with the cold. It was excitement. The thought of possibility. Life. Adventure.

Pete Wethers, Buffalo Bill and the Peaky Blinders feature in Andy Conway's Touchstone novel, Bright Star Rising *(along with Katherine Bright, Annie Oakley, Chief Red Shirt and a host of others). Buy it at andyconway.net where you can also claim your free* Touchstone *story,* The Reluctant Time Traveller, *in which Pete Wethers' granddaughter investigates the truth behind Kings Heath train station and the* Touchstone *universe.*

New Street Authors

New Street Authors is an open group that welcomes anyone willing to navigate the rough seas of self-publishing.

Its members publish across a wide range of genres, including literary fiction, science fiction, crime, fantasy, historical and children's; in diverse publications from paperbacks to ebooks to dyslexic-friendly print and encompassing numerous formats from novels, short stories, poetry, non-fiction and graphic novels.

◆

To find out more, and to join the mailing list for news of forthcoming releases, see **newstreetauthors.com**.